Dear Reader,

I've always been a
fondest memories of playing with my dolls while my
mother listened to "The Guiding Light" on the radio.
(Yes, the radio!)

By the time I started school, "Guiding Light" had moved
to television and I'll admit to occasionally sticking a
thermometer into my mother's morning tea, so it would look
as if I had a fever and could stay home to watch the latest
episode in the tumultuous life of the Bauer family. The trick
was to not keep the thermometer in the hot tea too long!

Years later, I'm still hooked on the Bauers, so when I
was invited to write for Temptation's Bachelor Arms
miniseries, it seemed natural to write a serial trilogy.
(With a sixty-year-old murder mystery thrown in to liven
things up.)

In *Never a Bride,* three friends—Cait Carrigan,
Lily Van Cortlandt and Blythe Fielding—come together
to celebrate Blythe's wedding.

The daughter of a much-married actress, Cait has no
intention of repeating her mother's mistakes. Marriage, she
vows, is not for her.

Until she meets Sloan Wyndham, a devastating screenwriter
with a dark and secret past. A man determined to change
her plans.

I hope you enjoy Cait and Sloan's stormy romance.
Stay tuned for Lily's story in Book Two of my wedding
trilogy—*For Richer Or Poorer.*

Happy Reading!

JoAnn Ross

BACHELOR ARMS

Come live and love in L.A. with the tenants of Bachelor Arms

Bachelor Arms is a trendy apartment building with some very colorful tenants. Meet three confirmed bachelors who are determined to stay single until three very special women turn their lives upside down; college friends who reunite to plan a wedding; a cynical and sexy lawyer; a director who's renowned for his hedonistic life-style, and many more…including one very mysterious and legendary tenant. And while everyone tries to ignore the legend, every once in a while something strange happens.…

Each of these fascinating people has a tale of success or failure, love or heartbreak. But their stories don't stay a secret for long in the hallways of Bachelor Arms.

Bachelor Arms is a captivating place, home to an eclectic group of neighbors. All of them have one thing in common, though—the feeling of community that is very much a part of living at Bachelor Arms.

BACHELOR ARMS

THE TENANTS OF BACHELOR ARMS

Ken Amberson: The odd superintendent who knows more than he admits about the legend of Bachelor Arms.

Connor Mackay: The building's temporary handyman isn't telling the truth about who he really is.

Caitlin Carrigan: For this cop, her career is her only priority.

Eddie Cassidy: Local bartender at Flynn's next door. He's looking for his big break as a screenwriter.

Jill Foyle: This sexy, recently divorced interior designer moved to L.A. to begin a new life.

Lily Van Cortlandt: This vulnerable, loving woman can forgive anything other than betrayal.

Natasha Kuryan: This elderly Russian-born femme fatale was a makeup artist to the stars of yesterday.

Gage Remington: Cait Carrigan's former partner is investigating a decades-old murder that involves the residents of Bachelor Arms.

Brenda Muir: Young, enthusiastic would-be actress who supports herself as a waitress.

Bobbie-Sue O'Hara: Brenda's best friend. She works as an actress and waitress but knows that real power lies on the other side of the camera.

Bob Robinson: This barfly seems to live at Flynn's and has an opinion about everyone and everything.

Theodore "Teddy" Smith: The resident Lothario—any new female in the building puts a sparkle in his eye.

JoANN ROSS
NEVER A BRIDE

Harlequin Books

TORONTO • NEW YORK • LONDON
AMSTERDAM • PARIS • SYDNEY • HAMBURG
STOCKHOLM • ATHENS • TOKYO • MILAN
MADRID • WARSAW • BUDAPEST • AUCKLAND

ISBN 0-373-25637-X

NEVER A BRIDE

Prologue

New Year's Eve
1933

LATER, GUESTS WOULD tell police there had been no foreshadowing that Hollywood's most infamous murder was about to take place.

It was nearly midnight. A white moon rose in a starspangled sky, creating a silvery path on the darkened waters of the Pacific Ocean below. From inside William Randolph Hearst's 118-room Palisades Beach Road house, came the sounds of a party in full swing. The glittering, starstudded evening belied the fact that the rest of the country was suffering in the grips of a depression. The light from hundreds of crystal chandeliers—imported from Europe—reflected off the women's glamorous silver and gold lamé evening gowns and created rainbows in the diamonds that blazed from their ears and wrists. The men were handsome in white tie, and those who weren't matinee idols had so much money, it didn't matter.

The scents of French perfume blended together, then wafted over the rooms like a fragrant cloud, mingling with blue smoke from Cuban cigars.

Crystal glittered, sterling gleamed, champagne flowed. Three jazz bands played in separate rooms and in one of the vast ballrooms, guests crowded around roulette and blackjack tables in the Havana-style casino created just for this gala night. Upstairs, in the many bedrooms, more intimate games of chance were taking place.

Outside, there was only the soft, unceasing sound of the incoming tide lapping against the glistening sand and the rustle of the sea breeze in the tops of the palm trees. Smoke from the smudge pots that nearby orange growers burned during these winter nights to warm their groves, wafted on the salt air. With the exception of that faint odor of smoke, it appeared to be another perfect night in Lotus Land.

A woman emerged from the mansion. A moment later, a man followed. Natasha Kuryan, watching from the shadows, recognized them immediately. Indeed, a person would have had to have spent the last year in a cave not to recognize the tempestuous Russian actress and her equally hot-tempered novelist husband.

Alexandra Romanov, of the deposed Czarist Romanovs and a direct descendant of Empress Catherine the Great, gossip columnist Louella Parsons had excitedly informed her readers, had been signed by Walter Stern, owner of Xanadu Studios, to counter the popularity of MGM's Dietrich and Garbo.

And it had worked, beyond Walter's wildest dreams. Critics and fans alike fell head over heels in love with the doe-eyed, sable-haired beauty whose exotic Russian looks provided a striking contrast to the lacquered blondes of the day.

Even Natasha, who was considered a beauty herself, could not help but admire the actress's flawless complexion. As a makeup artist at Xanadu Studios, it was Natasha's job to conceal movie stars' flaws. Alexandra—unfairly, Natasha often thought—had none to conceal.

Cannily taking advantage of the fact that women fantasized about being Alexandra, while men fantasized about getting her into their beds, Walter cast the actress in femme fatale roles, where her sultry love scenes inevitably raised temperatures in theaters all over America.

Indeed, the waterfall scene in her latest film—*Lady Reckless*—was so hot, one Hollywood wag professed that it was a miracle the celluloid film hadn't caught fire.

Unsurprisingly, Alexandra's movies routinely earned fines from the Hays commission. The National Legion of Decency boycotted her films. But since Xanadu was one of only two Hollywood studios ending the depression year in the black, Walter Stern cheerfully paid the fines, then laughed all the way to the bank.

Walter wasn't laughing the Christmas day Alexandra's personal life took an unexpected turn that rivaled her torrid screenplays. When the passionate, former Russian ballerina fell in love with Patrick Reardon, the tough-talking, hard-drinking, poker-playing western writer Walter had brought to Hollywood to pen the screenplay of his latest bestseller novel for Xanadu, Tinseltown pundits gave the romance a week. At the most.

Who wouldn't fall for the man, Natasha thought with a sigh. He was a true American cowboy, worlds more masculine than the make-believe movie kind. Whenever Patrick would show up on the back lot, women—even big-name stars—made fools of themselves to get his attention.

When Alexandra and Patrick shocked everyone by eloping on New Year's Day, the marriage was given a month.

That had been one year ago, and although Louella Parsons was hinting at recent tension between the couple, the current issue of *Life* magazine had just declared Alexandra and Patrick to be the most fascinating newlyweds on the planet, stripping the crown from that other famous Hollywood couple, Joan Crawford and Douglas Fairbanks Jr., popularly referred to as Cinderella and the Prince.

Living up to her ultraglamorous image, tonight Alexandra had definitely pulled out all the stops. She was barely clad in a dangerously low-cut white satin gown that flowed over her perfectly sculpted ballerina's body like mercury, shimmering like the inside of a sea shell in the streaming silver moonlight. The clinging satin dipped below her waist, leaving her smooth back bared but for the crisscross diamanté straps. It was obvious she was wearing nothing beneath the dress but resplendent, perfumed female.

She was wearing her thick sable hair loose and flowing; her trademark mermaid waves attractively ruffled by the sea breeze. In her right hand she held a champagne glass.

Her silver high heels were not made for walking in the sand; when she stumbled, Patrick, who'd easily caught up with her, took hold of her arm, as if to steady her.

Furiously shaking off his touch, she kept walking.

Equally furious, he grabbed her by the shoulders and spun her around.

Patrick was towering over his wife, looking huge and threatening. His broad shoulders strained the seams of his white dinner jacket, his dark hands curved around her pale white shoulders.

Besides rounding up cattle, he'd also been a boxer in his youth, earning the money which allowed him to write by knocking people out in western bars. When he'd first arrived in Hollywood, rumors had circulated that he'd killed a man—in Montana, or Wyoming, no one seemed to know which—with his bare hands. Since Reardon had refused to either confirm or deny the stories, they persisted.

Their faces were close together, but their taut angry poses were definitely not that of lovers. They exchanged words. Hot, angry words Natasha could not hear.

Suddenly, without warning, Alexandra slapped her husband across the cheek.

Patrick raised his own broad hand and for a long, suspended moment it looked as if he were actually on the verge of striking her back. Instead, he dropped his hand to his side.

Then, without another word, he turned and went striding back toward the house.

Alexandra called out to him, but her words were whipped away by the wind. She threw the champagne glass at his rigid, departing back.

Then she dropped to her knees in the soft sand and buried her face in her hands, the same way she had in her most recent film, when her married lover had chosen to return to his pregnant wife.

But this time Alexandra was not acting. From the way her bare shoulders shook, Natasha knew that her weeping was all too real.

She also knew exactly who'd orchestrated the problems Alexandra and her husband were experiencing. Up until now, she'd hesitated putting herself at risk. But witnessing the unhappy results of all that wicked, behind-the-scenes manipulating, Natasha vowed to tell Alexandra the truth.

But not tonight. This was too public a place to reveal such unsavory secrets.

Soon, she decided. Before the premiere.

The guests at the New Year's Eve Party never saw Alexandra Romanov again.

The following morning dawned bright and inappropriately golden. On what should have been her first wedding anniversary, the day before the premiere of her new movie, *Fool's Gold*, based on Patrick's screenplay, Alexandra was found dead in her dressing room in the sun-washed pink Spanish-style mansion she shared with her husband.

The day they'd moved into the home, shortly after their marriage, their neighbor, a contract writer at United Artists, had warned them that the house, which had been the scene of a mysterious death, was haunted.

Live in it and your greatest wish could be granted. Or your greatest fear realized.

Alexandra had been Russian enough to worry; her pragmatic western husband had laughed the story off, declaring it the product of the melodramatic screenwriter's warped imagination.

The coroner ruled Alexandra had been strangled.

Patrick was promptly arrested, tried and found guilty.

Two years later, on a dark moonless night while the hot Santa Anna winds blew in from the desert, making tempers flair and nerves crackle, Patrick Reardon was executed by the State of California for the first-degree murder of his wife.

1

Hollywood

LAND OF GLITTER and stardust. The Dream Machine. Film capital of the world where Garbo talked and Hepburn sparkled and Glenn Ford put the blame on Mame. Tinseltown, where the opulent glare of klieg lights once set the scene for glamorous star-studded movie premieres at Grauman's Chinese theater.

The problem, Cait thought, as she stepped around the strung out crack head who was throwing up atop Lee Marvin's star on the Walk of Fame, was that if ever a place failed to live up to its glitzy billing, it was Hollywood.

The mystique was definitely gone. The distinct scent hanging in the air was no longer that of fame and fortune, but pepperoni pizza. And despite the bronzed-edged stars embedded in the surface, the sidewalk she'd spent the past four hours strolling was definitely no yellow brick road.

A black clad guerrilla poet, sporting a purple mohawk, spiked black leather dog collar and a gold ring through his pierced nostril shouted out a rendition of his latest epic, drawing a small crowd of fascinated, yet wary tourists.

Nearby, a stunning black prostitute, wearing a tight red spandex dress and skyscraper, ankle-killing high heels, swayed seductively to Marvin Gaye singing from her boom box. Cait thought she looked a little like Diana Ross.

A late-model black Mercedes pulled to the curb in front of Cait. A moment later the passenger-side window rolled down. Displaying a definite lack of interest, Cait sauntered over.

"Yeah?" She cracked her gum and studied her long crimson fingernails.

"Do you want to go out?" the driver, a fifty-something guy asked. He wasn't all that bad looking, and the suit looked to be an Armani, but he was definitely no Richard Gere.

"Depends."

"On what?"

"On whether I decide I like you." She combed her hand languidly through her fiery hair and settled down to play verbal Ping-Pong. "What did you have in mind?"

"I have seventy-five dollars," he said.

"Good for you."

Instead of getting fed up and driving away, he smiled, revealing a row of straight white teeth which if not caps, had to have been bonded. "I like a lady with an attitude," he said. "Tell you what, sweetheart, this is your lucky night. I'll make it a hundred."

Rather than appear thrilled, Cait shrugged. "You're on."

When she heard the door unlock, she climbed into the car, settling down in the wide leather seat. "I've got a place around the corner," she said. "On Sunset."

When she named the motel, he said, "I know it." That, plus the fact he'd played the pickup game so well told Cait this was not his first time cruising the boulevard.

The Mercedes had the requisite phone, along with a fax. His nails had been buffed and his haircut, like his suit, carried the unmistakable look of Beverly Hills. Although she'd graduated from college with a minor in psychology, Cait figured she'd live to be a hundred and never figure out why guys who seemed to have so much going for them would be willing to pay for sex.

He slanted her a sideways glance. "I like your outfit."

"Thanks." She crossed her legs, giving him an enticing flash of thigh.

"You wearing anything under that skirt?" It was a leather micromini, red as sin and tight as a tomato casing.

"That's for me to know." When he put his hand on her bare leg, Cait gave him the smile she'd been withholding. "And for you to find out."

The promise had his fingers squeezing his approval in a way she knew would leave bruises.

He pulled the Mercedes into the parking garage, then followed her into the motel room, which did not pretend to be anything other than what it was. There was a bed, a rickety wooden chair and a wastebasket. Period.

The lumpy, too soft mattress sagged when he lay down on the bed. He folded his arms behind his head, crossed his legs at the ankles and said in a pleasant enough tone, "Why don't you strip for me?"

"What if I said dancing was extra?" Cait couldn't resist asking.

His eyes narrowed. "I'd suggest you not get greedy."

She smiled. "Just wondering." She reached behind her back, began to unzip the snug bustier, which, like her skirt was red leather, then stopped. "You know, you seem like a really nice guy, and it's not that I don't trust you, but—"

"Right." He lifted his hips, reached into his pocket, pulled out a gold money clip, peeled off five crisp new twenty-dollar bills and held them out to her.

"Thanks." She'd no sooner tucked the bills into the bustier when two men burst into the room from the adjoining bathroom.

"What the hell?" The man was on his feet in an instant, looking scared to death.

"Police," one of the intruders said, flashing his shield.

"Gotcha," Cait murmured with a rush of satisfaction. "You're under arrest," she announced. "For soliciting."

The man relaxed now that he knew he was not about to be robbed. Or worse. "Hell," he muttered in a resigned voice. "I want to call my attorney. To come get my car."

"No problem," Cait agreed readily. The vehicles were usually towed, but what the hell. If she owned a sixty-thousand dollar car, she wouldn't want it locked away in some police impound lot, either.

"What's your name, sweetheart?" he asked Cait.

"Officer Caitlin Carrigan," she said, expecting a complaint call to her division commander from the guy's Century City attorney. Knowing that it was a clean bust, she also volunteered her shield number.

But he didn't seem to be all that angry. If fact, if anything, the guy actually seemed more interested in her than ever. His blue eyes took a long judicious review of her.

"You're not a bad actress," he said.

Cait liked it when johns remained polite when busted. It made things easier for everyone. "Thanks."

"And you're really quite lovely. You remind me of a young Maureen O'Hara." Cait exchanged a quick glance with her partners, who rolled their eyes.

"That's nice of you to say," she murmured. Although parading around in public, dressed up like what her grandfather Carrigan would have called a floozie, hadn't bothered her, Cait was beginning to get decidedly uncomfortable with this conversation.

"It's the truth. I've always prided myself on having an excellent eye for beauty."

After four years as a cop, working the mean Los Angeles streets, Cait did not think there was anything left that could surprise her. She was about to be proven wrong.

"Do you have an agent?" Walter Stern III, owner of Xanadu Studios, asked with another of those dazzling, toothpaste commercial smiles. "I'm always looking for new talent."

BY THE END of her shift, Cait was not in the best of moods. She'd been working the Sunset Strip all afternoon and evening, and had even had to run back to the station to change into her other undercover outfit when the word got out that the lady in red was neither a lady nor a hooker, but a dreaded vice cop.

She had a pounding headache, her feet hurt, and if that wasn't bad enough, while she'd been out trying to make the streets safe, her mother—one of the few people in Hollywood who could still be considered an old-style movie star—had called the station, insisting on speaking with her.

"I tried telling her you were out on vice patrol," the dispatcher—a cigar-smoking, jaded thirty-year veteran who'd been assigned to desk duty after a heart attack—informed Cait. "But the lady doesn't take no for an answer all that easily."

"Tell me about it," Cait muttered. One of the few things she'd inherited from her mother—other than her looks—was a steely tenacity that had served her well as a cop. "I'll call her after I change."

"No need," he said. Cait didn't quite trust the sergeant's devilish grin. "I talked her into leaving a message." The grin had moved up to his eyes and Cait noticed that half the squad room had stopped to listen.

"I don't suppose you wrote it down?" she asked hopefully.

"Didn't have to," he said. "It wasn't that hard to remember." His grin widened ominously. "I was instructed to remind you that you're expected at noon on Sunday. For the Pet Parade Brunch."

The brunch was her mother's annual fundraiser for the local humane society and Cait had, admittedly, forgotten all about it. The eavesdropping cops burst into laughter. Brunch in Bel Air was not the way most cops spent their Sunday afternoons.

"Hey, Carrigan," her captain called out, "if you'd like, I can dye my wife's poodle pink. So you'll have something appropriate to take with you to this celebrity shebang."

That remark drew even more laughter which Cait answered with a pungent curse that even the most jaded street cops among them admired. Then she stomped downstairs to change into the jeans and T-shirt she'd worn to the station that morning.

The scene that greeted her did nothing to improve her mood. A man clad in the khaki uniform of the maintenance department was mopping the floor. The nearly full five-gallon bucket beside him revealed that the locker room had flooded.

"What happened?"

"Electrical problems," he explained laconically as he squeezed out the string mop.

"It looks more like plumbing problems to me."

"There was a short in the ancient electrical system that set off the overhead sprinkler system."

"Terrific." Cait made her way across the floor to her locker by stepping on dry patches. "If we don't get some money for improvements around here, the place is going to fall down around our ears."

"Every department's hurting," he said. "I haven't had a raise in two years, which doesn't much impress my kid's orthodontist when he expects me to pay for the braces that just bought his new boat."

Only half listening—everyone complained about the lack of public funding these days—Cait opened her locker. "Oh, hell!"

Her regular clothes were hanging next to her uniform and dripping water onto the metal floor of the locker.

"At least we know the sprinklers work," the man said.

"You've no idea how that relieves me," Cait said dryly as she realized that she had no choice but to drive home in her hooker outfit.

"No one held a gun to your head and forced you to be a cop," she reminded herself as she was subjected to a series of wolf whistles when she retrieved her red Mustang from the police lot.

Actually, most of the time, she loved her job. She loved the camaraderie of the squad, she loved the idea she was helping keep the city safe for innocent citizens, loved the fact that she never knew what was going to happen from one minute to the next and, most of all, she loved the sound of handcuffs clicking around the wrists of the bad guys.

But there were days, and this was one of them, when she wondered if just maybe she should have taken her high school counselor's advice and gone into nursing.

IT HAD BEEN SWELTERING in the dusty village of San Miguel for weeks. Tempers had flared and more than one fistfight had broken out. There had already been two brawls in the cantina just this morning, resulting in a stabbing incident that had sent one unlucky participant to the medical clinic. In a far corner, a man and a woman sat at a table, drinking tequila. Words were exchanged. The woman slapped the man's ruggedly handsome face, then stormed out of the cantina on a swirl of gauze skirts. Cursing violently, the man followed.

The air was pregnant with moisture. Thunder rumbled from fat gray clouds overhead. Because of the unrelenting heat and the impending storm, the street was deserted.

He caught up with her easily. When he grabbed hold of her arm, she furiously shook him off and continued walking.

His temper obviously at the breaking point, he gripped her by the shoulders and shoved her hard against the crumbling pink adobe wall of a deserted building.

"It's not what you think, dammit!" he shouted into her face.

"Isn't it?" She tossed her dark head. Her eyes glittered with barely repressed fury. "You promised me," she insisted. "You agreed it was the only way we could be together! Now that I've slept with you, now that you've gotten what you wanted, you're backing out on the deal."

"That's not true." He ran his broad hands over her shoulders. Her breasts. "I'll never get enough of you, baby." His flash fire anger metamorphosing into something just as hot, just as dangerous, he forced his knee between her legs.

"Dammit, Hunter—" Even as she complained, she began to rotate her hips.

"Shh." He bent his head and pressed his lips against her frowning mouth. The kiss was hot and long and deep. When it finally ended they were both breathing heavily.

"I told you," he rasped, his hands tangling in her hair, holding her gaze to his, "I've every intention of going through with the plan, Jillian. But it's not that easy."

"I know." Her hand moved between them and pressed against the placket of his jeans. "But nothing worth having is ever easy."

His body was straining against her hand. "He's an FBI agent, for chrissakes!"

"So are you," Jillian Peters reminded him silkily.

Sensing his surrender, she knelt and pressed her wet glossy lips against the faded denim. Giving in, as he'd known he would, Hunter Roberts closed his eyes and moaned as she drove him closer and closer to the brink.

The rain that had been threatening all day finally arrived on a deafening clash of thunderheads. It streamed over them, turning the red dust Jillian was kneeling in to mud.

When she began to unzip the jeans, Hunter grabbed her shoulders and pulled her to her feet again. The drenching cloudburst had rendered the sheer gauze dress nearly transparent. Her long legs were clearly visible, as were her nipples, which had pebbled from the sudden chill of the rain.

He pushed her back against the wall again, shoving her skirt up with one hand and unfastening his jeans with the other. Then, as the lightning flashed and the thunder boomed and the rain poured down, FBI Special Agent Hunter Roberts took her, standing up, in an alley of the sleepy border town where they'd first concocted the plan to murder her husband.

"CUT!" a voice shouted.

"Cut," the assistant director echoed.

On cue, on the back lot of Xanadu Studios, the rain abruptly ceased, the thunder silenced and the couple separated. A wardrobe woman rushed forward with thick terry robes and towels.

"That one had better be a take," Blythe Fielding muttered. "Much more of this and I'll get pneumonia."

"Much more and I won't be able to walk for a week," her costar, Drew Montgomery, complained.

She laughed at that as she rubbed her wet hair dry. "You're a newlywed, Drew. I'm amazed you have any energy at all."

He grinned. "I may be married, but a man would have to be dead not to respond to you, Blythe."

"You're still incorrigible." Her smile took the sting from her words.

"And you're still every bit as delectable as you were at seventeen."

They'd become teenage sweethearts while making a sophomoric summer camp slasher movie. Their brief romance had ended when the cameras had stopped rolling, but miraculously—in this town where lasting relationships were rare—they'd stayed friends.

"Sorry, Blythe, Drew," the director interrupted. "But we'll have to do it again."

"Dammit, Martin," Blythe protested, "I told you I have an important meeting this evening."

"I know." Martin Griffith's tone held as much irritation as hers. "But there was a damn boom in the shot. The clock's ticking down on this one, kids, and Stern is about ready to pull the plug."

"No great loss there," Blythe said beneath her breath.

Although the deal she'd recently cut with Xanadu studios required her to star in two films of the studio's choice for every one her own newly established independent production company made, Walter Stern III invariably insisted on casting her in these oversexed, underdressed, femme fatale roles.

"I heard that, Blythe," Martin said without rancor. "And for your information, this film is going to put my kid through Harvard—if we can get it in the can before he graduates from high school." Since Tyler Griffith was all of three years old, Blythe figured that even with all the bad luck they'd been having with the production, they might be able to—just barely—make that deadline.

"I have to make a telephone call," she said.

"Make it short. Candy's expecting you in makeup in five. With any luck, we can get this damn scene wrapped up before midnight."

Blythe entered the motor home that served as her dressing room. Sinking down on the flowered sofa, she dialed the now familiar number for Sloan Wyndham, the writer-director she was hoping to talk into writing the screenplay for her first independent project. When she got his answering machine, Blythe had no choice but to leave a message on the recorder. "Hello, Sloan? This is Blythe. Blythe Fielding," she tacked on unnecessarily.

This was the third time she'd had to change their scheduled appointment in the past week and each time she was afraid that Sloan, who wasn't exactly known throughout the movie community for his patience, was going to call the meeting off entirely.

"I'm terribly sorry, but I'm afraid we've run into a slight delay." Frustration, worry, contrition. Her tone radiated with all three as she dragged her hand through her thick dark hair. "I don't think I'm going to be able to make our six o'clock meeting. Would it be all right with you if we moved it to seven?"

Hoping for the best, but half expecting the worst, she said, "I'll ask my housekeeper to stay a little later to let you into the house, in case I'm not there when you arrive. Unfotunately, I think she's going deaf because she doesn't always hear the intercom, so let me give you the number of the gate alarm." She repeated the five-digit code three times.

She paused, as if waiting for an answer. "Once again, I apologize," she said, when none was forthcoming. "I'm usually irritatingly prompt. But things have been absolutely crazy here on the set. It's almost as if the film is jinxed." She desperately hoped he'd experienced similar problems on at least one of his own projects.

"Well, see you soon." She forced a bright note into her voice, as if to ensure his cooperation.

Hoping he'd think to call his machine before arriving at her house for their appointment, she replaced the receiver in the cradle, then made the mistake of glancing up at the mirror, where she'd taped an old black-and-white publicity still of Alexandra Romanov.

Posed in the glamour style of the times, the actress was lying on a satin chaise. She was wearing a clingy white silk negligee trimmed in marabou feathers that hugged her body like a lover's caress. Her hair was a thick sable cloud around her exquisite face, her lips were full and dark.

Although those voluptuous lips were curved in a staged, provocative smile, Blythe imagined she viewed sorrow in Alexandra's gypsy dark eyes.

The photo had been taken a mere week before her death. A week before her very public argument with her husband, novelist Patrick Reardon.

"What was it?" Blythe asked out loud. "What secret were you hiding that made you so sad?"

Blythe had given up questioning why she needed to know the answer. She only knew that for some reason beyond her understanding, it had become imperative for her to learn the truth.

She was still staring at the photograph ten minutes later when the beleaguered production assistant knocked on the motor home door, reminding her that they were waiting for her in makeup.

IN NO MOOD TO FACE all the boxes yet to be unpacked from her recent move to her new apartment in Bachelor Arms, Cait decided to drop by her best friend's for some pizza and girl talk.

Although Blythe Fielding's Beverly Hills neighborhood was a carbon copy of the one she'd grown up in, Cait enjoyed going to Blythe's home.

In contrast, whenever she was visited her mother's southern Colonial mansion in next door Bel Air, she always felt like a gangly, too skinny six-year-old with wild red hair and no front teeth.

The hills were definitely a peaceful respite from the bustling, grimy Hollywood district where she'd spent a long tiring day pacing the star-studded pavement. The trees were wearing new spring coats of bright green, the gardeners had planted more petunias and pansies and snapdragons than one could find at Disneyland, and miracle of miracles, you could almost breathe the air up here.

Cait rolled down her window as she passed a black Porsche Targa parked on the street. Automatically checking out the car's plate and tags, she took a deep breath of the evening air that carried a faint, bracing scent of the salt water drifting in on westerly winds from where Sunset ended at the ocean, and felt herself beginning to relax.

2

SLOAN WYNDHAM couldn't believe it. He dug deeper into his pocket and pulled out two gum wrappers, a library card that had nearly disintegrated after inadvertently going through a wash cycle, and some lint. But no slip of paper with the combination for Blythe Fielding's damn wrought iron gate.

That's when he remembered that he'd changed jeans after his afternoon run on the beach.

"Hell, all you have to do is think," he assured himself. "You wrote the damn number down. And checked it when she repeated it. So, try a little creative visualization."

He closed his eyes, took a deep breath and wished he'd paid more attention to Melissa Golden's constant attempts to get him more in touch with his subconscious.

The actress—and former lover—who'd starred in *Between Heaven And Hell*, the Oscar nominated film he'd written and directed about an idealistic nun and a burned-out cop tracking down a serial killer in downtown L.A., was every bit as intelligent as she was beautiful.

But not only was Melissa a method actress, which was bad enough in Sloan's opinion, she'd also never met a New Age philosophy she didn't embrace.

During the three months they'd been together, he'd witnessed her forays into the Daughters of Lemuria—female believers in a pre-Atlantean civilization allegedly located on the lost subcontinent in the Pacific, The Enlightenment of The Divine Mind, the Odyssey of the Inner Child, and the Universal Selfhood, just to name a few of the more esoteric disciplines. She'd also tried, unsuccessfully, to make him a believer.

"Okay. Here we go." He closed his eyes and concentrated. A moment later, he punched four numbers that seemed familiar.

Nothing.

"If at first you don't succeed . . ." He tried again.

Again, nothing.

Being familiar with Blythe Fielding's system—he'd had an identical one installed at his own Pacific Palisades house—Sloan knew that if he didn't hit the right combination of numbers on the third attempt, he'd trigger a series of ear-splitting alarms, which would also result in guards from a private security firm, as well as the Beverly Hills police, descending on him.

Although one of the things that immediately pegged him as a Hollywood maverick was Sloan's steadfast refusal to have a phone in his car, this was one of the few times he wished he'd given in to popular culture.

However, since he hadn't, he had no other choice but to drive back home, retrieve the damn piece of paper, then return here and open the gate. The additional delay, along with Blythe changing the time of the appointment in the first place, would result in his entire evening schedule being put hopelessly out of whack.

He was about to return to the Porsche when . . . "Hell," he decided, "If you don't try . . ."

Cait drove around the last hairpin turn on Benedict Canyon Drive before Blythe's house and brought the Mustang to a screeching halt when she saw the man climbing over the wrought iron gate.

Grabbing her 9 mm Glock from the glove compartment, she was out of the car in a flash.

"Police! Freeze."

Congratulating himself for nearly making it over the top of the gate without triggering the alarm or, more importantly, considering the row of deadly iron spikes at the top, endangering his ability to father future generations, Sloan turned his head and stared down in disbelief at the woman clad in the ultra short, skintight strapless dress.

"You have got to be kidding."

She sure as hell didn't look like any cop Sloan had ever seen.

Beneath the lacy, see-through dress, the outline of a skimpy hot pink bra and matching bikini panties was clearly visible. Her long legs were showcased by a pair of lacy white thigh-high nylons and white satin high heels that looked as if they'd come from Frederick's of Hollywood.

In a cascade of fiery hair that was tousled in a way that looked as if she'd just gotten out of bed was a white silk rose. Another rose, sewn to a white satin ribbon, adorned her neck.

In her right hand she was holding up what appeared to be a police shield. In her left was a 9 mm pistol. The contrast between the weapon and the white lace dress seemed enormous.

On second thought, taking in the slender curves displayed so enticingly beneath that white lace, Sloan decided that they were both, in their own way, pretty damn lethal.

As she watched the flash of male awareness in his eyes, Cait realized—too late—that her hooker patrol outfit did not exactly exude authority. Fortunately, her police pistol did.

"I want you to climb down from that fence very slowly," she said, her tone quiet, but forceful. "Then, I want you to place your palms against the brick wall."

For a fleeting moment Sloan thought about arguing, considered telling her who he was.

But before he could say a word, a memory flickered across the view screen of his mind, like a wartime flash-back—which, in its own way, it was.

He saw a phalanx of black-and-white police cars behind which were seemingly hundreds of cops. He saw the guns. Smelled the tear gas choking his lungs.

Then, as if he were watching it up on some oversize silver movie screen, he saw the man inside the building come running out. Sloan heard the deafening roar of all those guns being fired at the same time, saw the orange tracer of shots being fired.

No matter how many times that horrifying day replayed in his head, the shoot-out on that Portland, Oregon street seemed to take place in slow motion, like the final showdown scene in *Bonnie and Clyde*, when the infamous pair's crime spree was finally brought to an end.

In his case, when the acrid smoke finally cleared, fifteen-year-old Sloan Wyndham could see his father's bullet-riddled body lying dead on the sidewalk in a growing pool of blood.

He found himself getting icily furious even as he reminded himself that this lissome woman—this cop!—had nothing to do with his father's murder. "I'm coming down."

Adrenaline was coursing through Cait's system. It was the first time in her four years on the force that Cait had had reason to draw her sidearm in the line of duty. And unlike how a situation such as this was invariably depicted in fiction, she wasn't finding it a kick at all.

Contrary to the police bravado that thrilled audiences in all those *Lethal Weapon* and *Beverly Hills Cop* movies, as she watched him climb back down the gate, Cait was quite honestly and quite literally terrified.

She was terrified that she'd shoot this perp and suffer nightmares for the rest of her life. She was terrified that she wouldn't shoot him, in which case he'd have a weapon hidden away in his pocket and he'd shoot her. And she was also terrified that they'd shoot each other.

Her heart pounding painfully in her throat, Cait was more than a little relieved when he did as he was instructed and placed his hands obediently against the red brick wall that surrounded Blythe's property.

"All right." She moved to his right. "Wiggle your fingers." Her voice, she realized on some distant level of amazement, remained textbook calm and self-assured, belying the fact that her knees were knocking.

Realizing the dangers involved in arguing with a redhead who had a chip the size of the *Queen Mary* on her bare shoulder and a Glock 9 mm pistol in her hand, Sloan did as instructed.

She began to search him. "Very slowly, let me see your right hand.... Okay. Now your left." He wasn't concealing any razor blades, glass or dirt between his fingers. So far, so good, Cait thought.

"Put your palms back against the bricks. Turn your head to the left. And spread your legs. Wide."

Another burst of ice-cold fury, born in childhood and nurtured by his radical, counterculture parents throughout his formative years, shot through Sloan. Refusing to give this long-legged cop even the slightest excuse to shoot him in the back, Sloan managed, with a massive expenditure of effort, to conceal his anger as he did as he was told.

It was amazing, Cait thought, how things came back to you. As she began the frisking procedure she'd been taught in the Academy, her wildly beating heart slowed to a more normal rate.

Still holding her pistol in her left hand, she patted first his dark head, then his neck, then his arm, all the way to his hand and back up again, under the arm, across his chest, to his back, up and down, then around the waist.

Sloan could have written this scene himself. As a matter of fact, he had, several times.

"I can't wait for this next part," he drawled, knowing such sarcasm was risky, but furious enough that he could no longer allow her to throw her weight around with absolute impunity. Sloan had never been fond of authority. Official or otherwise.

"When I want you to talk, I'll ask you a question," Cait snapped, as she ran her hand over his groin, before moving down, then back up his legs.

Although the hooker clothes might be from Frederick's, her perfume was expensive. Expensive and sexy. But subtle. The kind that got under a man's skin. The kind designed to linger in a man's mind.

"Yes, ma'am."

His words, drawled in a deep baritone, were properly polite, but there was a mocking note to his tone. Switching her gun to her weaker hand, Cait repeated the process on his other side. All she managed to find were some gum wrappers, a ruined piece of cardboard that appeared to be a Los Angeles Public Library card and a key ring.

"All right," she said, once she'd determined that he wasn't carrying a weapon. "You can turn around. Slowly."

Although his clothes—a black Grateful Dead T-shirt and faded jeans—definitely hadn't come from Rodeo Drive and his thick, shaggy chestnut hair was in need of a trim, it crossed Cait's mind that he didn't look entirely out of place in the exclusive neighborhood. There was an air of confidence surrounding the man she wasn't accustomed to viewing in your run-of-the-mill burglar.

His expression gave nothing away.

"Would you care to explain what you were doing, climbing over that fence?"

"I don't suppose you'd believe that I left the combination at home in my other pants?"

She made a derisive sound.

He studied her frowning face, noted on some dispassionate level that she was stunningly beautiful, and gave a slow nod. "I didn't think so. But it *is* the truth."

"Do you know whose house this is?"

Sloan watched the mask of professional composure building, layer by layer on a complexion that was part honey, part cream. Reminding himself that while she might be a very appealing woman, she was first and foremost a cop, he tamped down the unwelcome tug of desire.

"Sure." He shrugged. "Blythe Fielding's. We had a meeting scheduled for this evening, but she was held up at the studio reshooting a scene. I'm Sloan Wyndham, by the way."

He tossed off the name with a casual air that suggested she'd recognize it immediately. Which she did. Damn. If he was telling the truth, Sloan Wyndham was important enough to get her called on the administrative carpet with a single phone call.

Even as she groaned inwardly, Cait schooled her expression to one of absolute controlled calm.

"I don't suppose you have any identification."

Sloan viewed the distress in her green eyes and felt a faint stir of pity. One he immediately squashed.

"You should know the answer to that," he said. "Did you feel a billfold while you were groping my ass? . . . Officer?" he tacked on with a respect they both knew was totally feigned.

If he'd been breaking into Blythe's home—which Cait was still not prepared to discount—he wouldn't tend to be carrying a wallet. Or any identification.

He watched the wheels turning in her head and decided to help her out. "I was running this afternoon on the beach. When I changed clothes, I forgot to put my ID in my pocket," he volunteered.

She'd done the same thing herself. Still... "Where do you live?"

When he gave her an address in Pacific Palisades, she lifted a tawny brow. "That's quite an afternoon run."

"It would have been. If I'd run it. But I drove here."

"Where's your car?"

"Around the corner. The black Porsche. You would've passed it."

She had. She'd even found it moderately interesting that it didn't have the vanity plates that were about as ubiquitous as security warnings in this neighborhood.

"There's no room to park in front of the gate," he elaborated. "And I didn't want to risk leaving it on this curve. So, when the housekeeper didn't answer the intercom and I realized I didn't have the combination, I parked the car down the road, walked back up here and decided to climb over the gate. Ms. Fielding assured me that the housekeeper would be home to let me in to wait for her."

"Why didn't you call Blythe at the studio and just ask her to give you the numbers again?"

"I don't have a phone in my car." At her sharp, disbelieving look, Sloan said, "Hey, check it out. You've already got the keys."

"I intend to do just that."

Cait gave him another long look, trying to decide what, exactly, to do with him. She didn't want to leave him here, in case he'd decide to go over the wall again.

She could take him with her, but what if this was all a lie and he decided to run for it? One of her biggest surprises was discovering, her first week on the job, that people had absolutely no compunction about lying to the police.

"You could always shoot me," he suggested helpfully, as he watched her sort out the dilemma.

Now that he had conquered his anger, which he would be the first to admit was a knee-jerk response, Sloan was beginning to find this scenario mildly interesting. Beauty and power made a dangerous—and intriguing—combination.

"That should keep me in my place."

He was smooth. Too smooth. The silky sarcasm in his tone and the masculine arrogance in his eyes tempted Cait to take him up on his suggestion.

"Somehow, I doubt that."

Her own tone was laced with an identical sarcasm. For some reason Sloan would think about later, when he wasn't wondering how in the hell she managed to sit down in that skintight dress, he'd figure out why he found it amusing.

"Got a point there," he said with a lazy shrug.

Once again his steely self-confidence told Cait that this was a man who belonged mingling with the rich and famous. Once again she reminded herself of what she'd learned in the Police Academy about not ever taking anything at face value.

"Don't you dare move so much as a muscle."

Sloan bestowed his most charming smile on her. "I wouldn't think of it."

The smile, meant to annoy, did exactly that. But on some distant, feminine level, Cait also had to admit that it was devastating. In the event he did turn out to be Sloan Wyndham, Cait wondered if Blythe was truly planning to work with him.

And if so, what Blythe's stuffy, social-climbing physician fiancé would have to say about the collaboration.

Keeping her gun trained on him—which made her feel a little ridiculous, but she assured herself she'd feel a lot more ridiculous if she ended up letting some lying, thieving perp get away—she reached into her car and retrieved her handcuffs.

"You realize, of course," he said, when he saw what she had in her hand, "that you're going to end up apologizing for this." And damn was he going to enjoy watching her do it!

"If you're not who you say you are, I won't have to apologize for anything." She took his right wrist and cuffed it to the gate. "And if you really are Sloan Wyndham, next time you find someone climbing over *your* driveway gate in the Palisades, instead of 911, try calling the Screenwriters' Guild."

She turned on those ridiculously high heels and as she marched away around the hairpin curve to where he'd left the Porsche parked, it crossed Sloan's mind that for a stormtrooper, the lady cop had a very nice ass.

Cait swore. The Porsche, as he'd told her, was registered to Sloan Wyndham. And the address *was* in Pacific Palisades. Of course, she reminded herself, that didn't mean that the man she'd caught climbing over Blythe's gate was the owner of this car.

But she'd bet her shield he was.

As she walked back up the street, Cait only hoped it wouldn't come to that.

Already twenty minutes late for her rescheduled appointment with Sloan, Blythe hoped yet again that stories of the talented screenwriter's impatience would prove to be exaggerated. The project she'd planned for her fledgling production company's first film was already turning out to

be more difficult than she could have imagined. If she didn't
sign a writer soon . . .

No! Blythe refused to think that she might not be successful. Somehow she would convince Sloan Wyndham to
write her screenplay. And she would make this movie that
had become what could only be described as an obsession.

As she approached her driveway, Blythe couldn't believe
her eyes. She stared at the man handcuffed to her gate.

"Sloan? What on earth?"

"Hello, Blythe," he said with an amazingly casual air for
a man in his position. "How about doing me a favor and
putting a good word in with Dirty Harriet?"

"Dirty Harriet?" Blythe glanced around, wondered why
she hadn't seen the familiar red Mustang when she'd first
pulled up and decided that her attention had been immediately captured by the picture Sloan made handcuffed to
her gate. "Oh, no. I take it you've met Cait."

On cue, Cait came around the bend, viewed the two of
them talking like old friends and could practically see her
career going up in smoke.

"Don't tell me that outfit is regulation," Blythe greeted
her.

"It's a long story," Cait muttered. She glared over at
Sloan, who gave her a bland I-told-you-so look in return.
"I don't suppose you can ID him?"

"Of course I can. It's Sloan Wyndham. What I haven't
determined is what he's doing handcuffed to my gate."

"Actually," Sloan said before Cait could answer, "the officer was only protecting your property, Blythe. I left your
combination at home, so I decided to climb over the gate.
Under the circumstances, Cait's response was absolutely
justified."

Cait had expected him to inform her that he was on his
way downtown to file a citizen's complaint. Perhaps even

threaten a lawsuit. She knew she should be relieved. But for some reason, having Sloan Wyndham defend her actions irked. Especially when his deep voice made her name sound like a caress.

Irritation scored a line between her tawny brows. "The name is Officer Carrigan."

"I like Cait better."

"Tough," she practically snarled through gritted teeth as she moved to release him.

Lord she smelled good! Too good for a cop. He had a sudden urge to skim a finger over one of those bare shoulders. "You sure you want to do this?"

Surprised, she looked up him and found herself momentarily caught off guard by the unexpected humor—and something far more dangerous—in his eyes. "Do what?"

"Release me." Touching wouldn't be enough, Sloan realized as he was hit with an even stronger urge to sink his teeth into that fragrant flesh. "Do you know how many people in this town would love having me as a captive audience?"

The maddening thing was it was all too true. "You're forgetting something." She yanked the cuffs off. "I'm a cop. Not an actress."

"You could be."

His smooth flattery, which reminded her of her earlier encounter with Walter Stern, only irritated her further. Cait supposed that the line probably worked with most of the women of Sloan Wyndham's acquaintance.

But not her.

Definitely not her.

"Gee, Mr. Wyndham," she cooed on an eager, breathless little voice, "are you saying that if I'm a good girl and treat you nice, you could actually make little old me a star?"

She was gazing adoringly up at him through her lashes. When she provocatively licked her glossy pink lips, Sloan felt dual twinges of humor and desire.

"With your own series," he agreed, playing along. Knowing better, but unable to resist, he tugged on a wayward bright curl. "Lady Law." His gaze skimmed down her body. "If you wore that dress in the pilot, sweet Cait, ratings would go soaring through the roof."

He was close. Much too close. Cait yanked her hair loose and backed away. "I was working undercover. On Sunset."

He nodded. "I figured that was the case, since, as Blythe has already pointed out, that outfit isn't exactly regulation."

His gaze drifted down to those amazing legs. "Lord, I'll bet business was booming." Back to her face, which, surrounded by that wild, fiery mane of hair reminded him of a ravished Irish milkmaid. "You undoubtedly had cars backed up all the way to the Hollywood Freeway."

The unfortunate reality of real-life prostitutes was that they never looked like they did in the movies. Cait looked even better, which should have been a tip-off right there. But then again, Sloan considered, he doubted many of the johns cruising the strip would have been able to resist such delectable bait. Putting this luscious lady on the street seemed almost unfair.

"It does seem, though, as if you could be accused of entrapment."

Since joining the Vice Special Detail, Cait had heard much the same thing from defense lawyers too many times to count. Irritating as it was to be accused of entrapment in court, it was even more annoying coming from a man known for his numerous and short-lived romantic liaisons.

"I should have shot you when I had the chance."

"Too late." He reached out and touched the earring that dangled like a gleaming chandelier from her lobe. "I've got a witness, Officer Cait."

It was then Cait belatedly remembered Blythe. She glanced around and found her best friend leaning against her car door, arms folded, eying them both with interest. And amusement.

"Well, you have a meeting. And I've got to get home." As Sloan continued to grin at her with that arrogant male smugness, Cait decided it was past time to leave.

She was halfway to the Mustang when she remembered her mother's message and turned back to Blythe. "You are coming Sunday, aren't you?"

"Sunday?" Blythe repeated blankly.

"The Pet Parade Brunch?"

Given her choice, the glitzy celebrity affair would not have been Blythe's first choice of a way to spend a rare day off. But knowing how difficult it was for Cait to appear in public with her glamorous, larger-than-life mother, she decided she had no choice but to accompany her to the charity brunch.

"I wouldn't miss it for the world," she lied.

Cait laughed. And thought about how she was going to miss her best friend.

Of course Blythe was continually promising that her upcoming marriage to the Beverly Hills plastic surgeon would have no effect on their friendship.

Cait only wished she could believe that.

There were also days when she wished she could believe in the tooth fairy and Santa Claus.

But if there was one thing her twenty-five years on this planet and her own parents' serial weddings had taught her, it was that marriage always changed things. And not for the better.

3

BLYTHE HAD NEVER WORKED with Sloan Wyndham, but she had met him socially. She'd also followed his work, beginning eight years ago with his first film, *The Arlington Seven*, about a violent Vietnam era protest group. After winning best documentary at the Sundance and Telluride film festivals, it had gone on to win honors and industry attention at Cannes.

Although his successive projects achieved commercial success, it was obvious that he'd not surrendered his vision to profits. His latest film was a riveting, dramatized day in the life of war-torn Sarajevo, interspersed with rough cuts from the 1984 Olympics in that same city. *Keepers of the Flame* was visual and dramatic and each of the three times she'd seen it, Blythe had left the theater emotionally drained.

You didn't have to be a graduate of UCLA's film school to see that Sloan Wyndham had an agenda. His stories were all modern day morality plays, but delivered with such taut control and irony, they never seemed to preach.

Blythe could tell for herself that he was talented. She'd heard stories of his impatience and fierce independence, which routinely landed him in hot water with studio executives. There were also rumors of a hedonistic bachelor lifestyle.

She had no problem with independent individuals. And having certainly been known to be impatient with slackers herself, she couldn't fault Sloan Wyndham for that character trait.

As to his reputed hit-and-run romantic life, since he was certainly handsome enough—with his lean hard body, intense whiskey brown eyes and shaggy, thick chestnut hair—to have earned his living on the performing side of the camera, Blythe suspected at least some of the rumors concerning his romantic entanglements might be true.

However, having grown up in a town where outrageous behavior was often the norm, she was a bit like that proverbial British aristocrat who didn't really care what people did, so long as they didn't do it in the middle of the road and frighten the horses.

She had expected to spend a few minutes exchanging pleasantries, the small talk that was so much a part of deal making in Hollywood. She'd chosen the sunroom for their meeting, hoping that the comfortable, leafy environs overlooking the rose garden and swimming pool would be a conducive atmosphere for their meeting.

Displaying his legendary impatience and his maverick streak, she'd no sooner served their drinks—an imported dark beer for him, a California chardonnay for her—when Sloan, eschewing polite social conversation, immediately got down to brass tacks.

"I don't understand what it is you want from me," he said.

"I thought I'd made that perfectly clear when we'd first set up this meeting." Blythe took a sip of her wine and reminded herself that she was the producer. *She* should be the one interviewing *him*, not the other way around. "I'd like you to write a screenplay."

"About Alexandra Romanov." He did not sound as if he were chomping at the bit for the opportunity.

"That's right."

"The thing is—" he braced his elbows on the arms of the white wicker chair "—you should probably understand right off the bat, the way I work.

"Coming up with stories isn't a problem for me. The trick is to find the idea behind the story. It can be political or social or just some new way to get to the truth.

"I've always believed that for a film to be successful, it has to affect thinking, it has to have an impact on the audience's concept of life."

"That's pretty much what I believe, as well." Blythe desperately hoped he wouldn't point out that her films for Xanadu had been less than epic quality. The problem was, Walter Stern III had the money she needed; if she wanted to play on his court with his ball, she had to play the game by Stern's rules.

Normally, Sloan wouldn't have wasted his time even discussing this project. But he'd always thrived on challenge. And for him, the greatest challenge of all was transforming real stories into a movie. He believed that films were forever, and that by taking an actual event and giving it realistic vitality on the screen, he made that truth endure.

One problem he'd been having since Blythe's out-of-the-blue telephone call was exactly how much truth the lady was looking for. If she expected him to turn Alexandra Romanov's tragic death into another one of those exploitation films she was famous for starring in, the kind that would be forgotten before the credits rolled across the screen, she was definitely talking to the wrong screenwriter.

"I have a couple of questions."

His gaze locked onto hers. Uneasy, but loath to show it, she nodded and willed herself to calm. "All right."

"First of all, why me?"

That was easy. Blythe allowed herself to relax slightly. "Because I've seen all your films. You have a way of getting to the truth, no matter how unpleasant, and illuminating it. Each time I've left the theater feeling as if I've just been given a close-up look at something very personal."

It was, Sloan admitted, a perfect answer. He wondered if she had any idea exactly how personal one of those films had been, then decided she didn't. He'd hid his tracks too well.

"Which brings us to my second question," he said. "Although it's nothing I can put my finger on, from our phone conversations over these past two weeks, I have the feeling this project is very personal to you."

"It is," Blythe admitted.

"Why?"

Good question, Blythe admitted. "I don't know."

He gave her another one of those long silent looks that made her want to squirm in her chair. Sloan noted her nervousness. And her fatigue that spoke of long days at the studio and longer nights working on this project. He also recognized a streak of stubbornness that was more than a little familiar.

"Okay," he said finally, deciding not to press, "I can buy that...."

"Last question—are you hiring me to write a screenplay? Solve a murder? Or right a sixty-year-old wrong?"

It was a question she'd been asking herself for weeks. And although so many acquaintances had already warned her that she was tilting at windmills, some deep-seated instinct she'd learned to trust told her that Patrick Reardon had not killed his glamorous movie star wife.

"I think," Blythe said slowly, honestly, "all three."

She watched him mull over her answer, refusing to flinch as those direct brown eyes searched her face as if looking for clues.

When she didn't view the skepticism she'd expected to see in his steady gaze, she decided to lay her final cards on the table. "I've been thinking about this project for a long time."

Obsessed was, perhaps, a more accurate word, but she didn't want him to worry that he was being asked to work with a crazy woman. "And I'm convinced that you're the only man who can find the truth beneath the scandal."

Despite the obvious obstacles—beginning with the little fact that Hollywood lore had tried, convicted and literally executed Patrick Reardon more than sixty years ago—or perhaps, because of all the inherent problems, Sloan found himself tempted to sign on to the project.

He knew Blythe would get this film made, one way or the other. The only question remaining was whether he'd be part of the process.

"I've always liked mysteries," he mused aloud.

He was looking out the window, but from his faraway gaze, Blythe suspected it was not the sun setting over the Pacific he was seeing, but some distant event visible only to him.

She was right. "So—" he turned back toward Blythe "—you said you had some clippings?"

She nodded and reached into the leather attaché case she'd brought home from the studio with her and pulled out a slim manila envelope. "Unfortunately, I couldn't find very much."

The lack of information about the actress in the Xanadu studio archives had proven both puzzling and annoying. After all, Alexandra Romanov's films had been the primary source of income for the studio during the Great Depression.

For a business reputed to be built on creativity, Blythe knew, all too well, that it was money that kept the Dream Machine oiled and running. Considering the box office gate during Alexandra's heyday, she would have expected a shrine to have been erected to the actress.

"I did manage to come up with these clippings in the newspaper annex of the library," she said, handing them over to him. "I'll admit there doesn't seem to be a great deal of information about Alexandra's life before her death, but—"

"Don't worry about that." Realizing he'd responded too curtly, Sloan softened his tone and his expression. "If these pique my interest, I can always dig around in the studio morgue myself."

"I'm afraid that studio files aren't available for public viewing." Although she certainly didn't want to discourage the man before he'd agreed to write her screenplay, Blythe felt she was obliged to be honest about how little he'd have to work with.

"Don't worry about that." He waved off her warning with a lazy flick of his wrist. "It just so happens that I've got friends in high places." He didn't elaborate, leaving Blythe to wonder who, exactly, might be willing to break Walter Stern's sacrosanct rules.

Surely not Alice, studio archivist. The woman who'd recently celebrated her thirty-fifth anniversary working at Xanadu protected her precious files like a dragon in a video game guarded the royal treasure.

"There's one more thing."

Somehow, Blythe had a feeling there would be. "What's that?"

"If I do decide to take this project on—and I'm not saying I will—I'll want to direct."

Blythe told herself that knowing his reputation for wanting to maintain ultimate control of a project, she should have foreseen this development. Which could turn out to be a problem, if his artistic vision proved at odds with her own view of the film.

A producer tinkering around with a writer's screenplay was not unheard of in her business. Telling a director how to direct was an entirely different matter.

"I don't know if—"

"Let me try to explain it to you," he said, cutting her off again. "For me, a screenplay is like a huge block of marble. It's wonderful and promising, but easily ruined. I've always viewed the director's role to be that of a sculptor, chiseling away at the stone, ultimately setting the vision— and the truth—free."

His jaw and his eyes hardened in a way that made her realize this was not a negotiating point.

"I categorically refuse to expend creative energy on a story only to let some guy with a chain saw loose on it."

Although she understood his concern, Blythe took offense at his disparaging tone. "I can see your point," she allowed coolly. "However, I certainly wasn't planning to hire some hack."

Sloan liked the way her back stiffened when she was irritated. He also liked the way she stood up to him. Since his string of successes had put him in the upper echelon of hot properties in Hollywood, making him one of a few "bankable" writer-directors, most women—hell, most people— tended to fawn in his presence.

Sloan was well aware of the fact that one flop would cause those same people to instantly forget his name.

"I'm sure whomever you're considering is competent," he said. "Hell, maybe even brilliant. But it doesn't matter to me. Because the truth is, Blythe, you could hire the best damn director in the business.

"But when the picture's finished, whatever was born from that beginning block of marble would be his or her vision. Not mine."

"That makes sense," Blythe agreed slowly. From what she'd witnessed thus far, she wondered if Sloan was as difficult to work with as she'd heard and decided that it didn't matter. She wanted to get her picture made right. And she still believed he was the man to do it.

"Look, all this is still a bit premature," he said. "Why don't we have this discussion after I read these clippings? Then I can let you know whether or not I'm interested in signing on."

It was not the answer she'd wanted. But she knew it was the only answer she was going to get for now. Reminding herself that patience was suppose to be a virtue, and forcing herself not to give him an arbitrary deadline, Blythe reluctantly agreed. As she walked him to the door, then stood in the redbrick driveway, watching the Porsche drive away, Blythe was frustrated by the fact that she had not a single clue as to Sloan's feelings. For a town where egos and emotions were openly displayed, she found his way of keeping his thoughts to himself both irritating and refreshing.

"I CAN'T BELIEVE you're going to be working with that oversexed wunderkind," Cait said as she and Blythe drove to the Pet Parade Brunch on Sunday. They'd decided, for friendship's sake, as much as convenience, to drive to the garden party together.

"Actually, I think Sloan's reputation may be exaggerated," Blythe argued mildly. "He was quite the gentleman during our meeting. Really," she insisted when Cait shot her a disbelieving look. "I think we're going to be able to work quite well together."

"That's probably what Little Red Riding Hood said about the Big Bad Wolf," Cait muttered.

Having grown up in the business, Cat knew firsthand about handsome, charming rogues. After all, her father, whom she truly adored, could have set the standard for such Hollywood rakes.

Deciding that it wasn't her responsibility to defend the screenwriter's admittedly less than sterling reputation, Blythe didn't respond to Cait's sarcasm.

"Speaking of oversexed," she said, "that really was quite an outfit you were wearing the other day." Although the reference brought up her humiliating encounter with Sloan Wyndham, something Cait had unfortunately been thinking about far too much these past days—and nights—she couldn't help but grin.

"Didn't you think it was me?"

"Actually, I thought you looked a bit like Madonna, in the old days."

"Bingo. Give the lady a Kewpie doll. That was my *Like a Virgin* outfit."

The wicked grin reached all the way to her eyes and caused gold facets to radiate from the bright green depths. "Since you still haven't gotten around to picking out a wedding dress, I'll let you borrow it for your upcoming nuptials."

"Alan would love that." Blythe's dry tone said otherwise.

Cait shook her head in frustration. "Have you noticed that ever since you started dating the good doctor, you've gotten awfully stodgy?"

"Stodgy?"

"A six-letter word meaning boring. Sometimes it's hard for me to believe that you're the same adventurous, fun-loving girl who glued three red silk roses onto a bikini and went to the Sigma Chi halloween party as a Rose Bowl float."

Blythe didn't know it was possible to grin and groan at the same time. If Alan ever found out about that stunt . . .

"That doesn't count. We were in college." She firmly believed that the president should declare an official national amnesty for all the stupid stunts people pulled during the four intense, often insane years they spent away at university.

"Are you telling me that if you'd been engaged to Alan at the time, you still would have done it?"

The question was a good one, Blythe admitted reluctantly. "Probably not."

Cait folded her arms. "I rest my case. I also don't think you should make such snap judgments about that dress," she advised. "As boring as the doc can be, I doubt there's a man alive who doesn't fantasize about his woman in a trashy, sexy outfit like that one. It works like Love Potion Number Nine whenever I wear it out on Hollywood Boulevard."

"Alan is not the kind of man to pick up women on the street."

"Believe me, you can't always tell. Although in the doc's case, I'd probably have to agree with you," Caitlin admitted. "But I'll bet you'd never guess in a million years who I busted the other day."

"I don't believe it," Blythe said when Cait revealed her recent celebrity arrest. "Walter Stern actually offered to pay you for sex?"

"I told you," Cait said with a shrug, "you just never know. What was even more amazing was the way he hinted that if I played my cards right, I could have an audition at Xanadu."

Cait frowned as she remembered Sloan's similar remark when she'd almost arrested him and wondered why men in this town couldn't get it through their heads that the bad old days of the casting couch were over. Her frown darkened as she decided the sad truth was that though sleeping your way to the top of the studio might not be as prevalent as it once was, trading sex for parts undoubtedly happened more times than she cared to know.

"But Walter has a gorgeous young wife," Blythe argued.

His fourth. Some brainless airhead with a silicon enhanced Barbie doll body, who'd recently been signed to play the part of a moll in a mobster picture, Blythe recalled.

"Hey, most of the guys we bring in are married. Which is one more reason I have no intention of ever tying the knot."

Having been Cait's best friend since childhood, Blythe was all too familiar with Cait's aversion to marriage. In truth, she could even understand it, given the fact that Cait's mother, Natalie Landis had been married seven times at last count, and Devlin Carrigan, her screenwriter father had gone to the altar five times. Or was it six?

Whichever, the thought of her best friend fated to go through life alone, just because of her parents' failed romances, made Blythe sad.

"You certainly can't judge all men by the ones who solicit hookers," Blythe pointed out.

"Right. Let's talk about the child molesters and wife beaters and rapists."

"You really do need to get into another line of work." Blythe wondered as she so often did, how Cait could remain so unrelentingly upbeat when she spent her days mucking around in society's sewer.

"And give up playing cops and robbers?" Cait shook her head. "Never happen. But you know," she said, "when you talk like that, you sound depressingly like my mother.

"She's still telling all her movie star friends that the only reason her daughter is running around in an LAPD uniform is because I'm researching a role for some television series that only exists in her mind."

"I'm sorry I sounded that way," Blythe said. The last thing she wanted was to hurt Cait's feelings. "You know I've always respected your career choice. Although," she admitted, as she turned into Natalie Landis's sweeping driveway, "I certainly can't imagine doing it myself."

"Different strokes," Cait said with renewed good humor. "So, when does the nose doc get back to town?"

Alan had been gone for the past ten days at a medical convention in Bonn, and although Blythe truly missed him, one thing she'd definitely not missed were their arguments regarding her workaholic lifestyle.

"I've told you time and time again not to call him the nose doc," she complained lightly, knowing Cait's feelings about Hollywood's obsession with artificially enhanced beauty. Of course it helped, Blythe considered, that Caitlin was naturally stunning.

"He'll be back in town Wednesday morning. We're scheduled to have dinner with the retiring director of surgical services Wednesday night."

"Boy, the guy must have a lot of energy," Cait conceded. "I'd be too jetlagged out after flying all that way back from Europe to go out and make party conversation."

"So would I. But Alan didn't have any say in setting the date."

"And of course he can't not go," Cait guessed. "Since he's undoubtedly lobbying for his retiring superior's job.

"He *is* the most qualified," Blythe said loyally. And although she knew that she could be considered obsessive from time to time—like now, with her Alexandra project—she was a piker compared to her fiancé.

Alan Sturgess played hospital politics the same way he played tennis. To win.

Blythe's unusually sharp tone had Cait slanting a curious look her way. "I didn't say he wasn't," she said. "Just because I don't think the guy's right for you doesn't mean I can't acknowledge his medical talents, Blythe."

Uncomfortable at having snapped at her best friend, and knowing that there was no love lost between Cait and Alan, Blythe was relieved when their arrival at Natalie Landis's Bel Air estate precluded further discussion.

A visitor to the Colonial mansion would undoubtedly feel like a time traveler to the Old South. Although Cait hated the memories her childhood home represented, still she could appreciate the southern beauty of the gleaming white six-pillared mansion. The curving entrance drive flowed onto a velvety green sweeping lawn and magnificent gardens that provided a dramatic landscape.

The inside of the mansion was as dazzling as the exterior. A fantasy come true that was almost as glamorous as its movie star owner. Settings swept opulently from soaring gilt-framed ceilings, creamy Italian marble flowed underfoot, an ornately gilded curving staircase suitable for a fairy-tale princess-to-bride float down romantically. Museum quality paintings adorned silk-draped walls, billowing treatments framed the tall windows.

The formal gardens were in full bloom, orchids floated atop the azure waters of the tiered swimming pool. A string quartet from the Hollywood Symphony played Bach and Beethoven while Hollywood's heaviest hitters nibbled on canapés, sipped mimosas and mingled and gossiped.

The affair was Natalie Landis at her best. There was enough glitz and glamour gathered around the sparkling pool to fill the Hollywood Bowl. More stars than the Griffith Planetarium.

How many parties like this had she been to in her life? Cait wondered. Hundreds? Thousands? And she hadn't enjoyed any of them.

"Relax," Blythe advised Cait under her breath as they joined the gala gathering. "You look like a virgin brought to the slaughter."

"I hate these damn things," Cait said between clenched teeth.

"I'm not all that wild about them myself," Blythe admitted. She flashed a smile at the television reporter who was covering the charity brunch for "Entertainment Tonight". "But when in Rome . . ."

"I wish I *were* in Rome. Anywhere but here."

Blythe waved at a former NFL quarterback who'd surprised all the critics by proving himself to be a very good dramatic actor. "It'll be over before you know it."

"That's undoubtedly what the chaplain tells death row inmates while they're getting their heads shaved," Cait countered.

There had been a time when Blythe had wondered why it was that although she could tolerate Hollywood's more superficial moments, on those rare occasions when her best friend succumbed to Natalie's not inconsiderable will, Cait always seemed like a fish out of water.

It hadn't been until one memorable night, when all of Cait's various stepfathers and stepmothers unexpectedly showed up at the same party, that Blythe had realized Cait's insecurities stemmed from her lack of stability during her important formative years.

Both Cait and Blythe had grown up in the movie business. They'd attended the same schools from kindergarten through college. They were both intelligent and attractive. They both had careers they loved.

The difference had been that Blythe's parents had provided a family that could have been the prototype for a 1950s television program. As an entertainment attorney, David Fielding had worked a normal nine to five job while his wife combined running their home and taking care of their daughter with her charity work.

In contrast, Natalie Landis and Devlin Carrigan had spent their entire lives—and, distressingly, Cait's—in a seemingly nonending series of tempestuous relationships.

Cait had been at the Pet Parade Brunch less than five minutes when her mother's butler informed her that she had a telephone call from police headquarters. From the disapproving tone in his properly British voice, she guessed he shared his employer's distaste for her chosen profession.

"Thank you, Malcolm." Cait forced a smile at the man who, during his entire seventeen years in Natalie Landis's employ, she'd never once seen crack even a hint of a smile in return. "I'll take it in the library."

"Wherever you wish, Miss Caitlin." He nodded brusquely, then walked away, his spine and his attitude as stiff as his starched white shirtfront.

Wondering as she so often did how it was that her mother had been able to maintain such a long-term relationship with her butler, when she went through marriages like tissues during the cold and flu season, Cait shook her head and wove her way through the crowd.

The library, like the foyer, boasted a towering, two-story ceiling. Exquisite Persian carpets floated atop the black marble floor. Leather bound books, which looked as if they'd never been opened, lined the walls.

The old-fashioned style telephone on the cherry Queen Anne desk was antiqued and appropriately gilded. Although she routinely turned on her call forwarding whenever she left her home, Cait was definitely not accustomed to receiving calls from division headquarters.

"This is Detective Andretti, in the fugitive squad," the male voice on the other end of the line informed her brusquely. "We've got a little problem here, Officer. And we think you may be able to help."

"I'd certainly be happy to try, sir," she said trying to keep her tone briskly professional as a frisson of excitement shot through her. "What is it?"

"I'd prefer not to discuss it on the phone," he said, causing her interest to skyrocket. "Could you come downtown, at say, three o'clock?"

"Three o'clock is fine, sir," she agreed without hesitation.

"We'll see you then," he said, sounding as if he'd expected no other answer.

"Don't worry about it," Blythe said when Cait told her about the change in plans. "We'll simply leave a little early so you'll have time to change into your uniform."

Patience had never been Cait's long suit and it wasn't now. For the next two hours, as she forced herself to circulate and exchange small talk with these people she'd known all her life, she couldn't help wondering what the fugitive squad could possibly want with her.

Her mind continued to reel off endless scenarios, trying each on for size, then discarding them, like a dress that didn't quite fit.

Later, she would tell herself that her intense concentration on the phone call from the head of Los Angeles Police's fugitive squad was why she hadn't noticed Sloan Wyndham's arrival at the party.

4

BLYTHE HAD NEVER LIKED Walter Stern. Even before Cait's revelation about his solicitation arrest, she'd found him smarmy. But just because she didn't like the man didn't mean she couldn't work with him. At least that's what she'd been telling herself.

But lately she had the feeling that he was doing everything he could to deter her from making the film about Alexandra Romanov in the first place.

Which didn't make any sense, she considered. Unless he was worried about Xanadu Studios being portrayed in an unattractive light.

Taking advantage of his appearance at the brunch, she was attempting, unsuccessfully thus far, to talk him into granting her additional access to his grandfather's and father's old archives files when Sloan approached.

"We need to talk," he said without preamble.

Once again his curt tone reminded her that he was reputed to be difficult. But still Blythe found herself hoping he'd accept her proposal.

"I'm a little busy at the moment." Refusing to grant him the upper hand, she purposefully made her tone chilly.

He smiled at that, a slow, remarkably sexy smile that warmed those whiskey brown eyes and had Blythe reminding herself she was an engaged woman.

"Sorry. I tend to get impatient when I'm excited about a story."

Hope flared. Enough that Blythe missed the studio head's stiffening beside her. "Are you saying—"

"I'm interested. Hell, I'm more than interested."

Blythe felt her mouth go suddenly dry. "And that is?"

"Your project has dynamite potential, Blythe. Factor in you playing the part of Alexandra, and it can't miss. I'd be a fool to turn down the opportunity."

Relief shuddered out on a long breath. "Thank you."

He shrugged in a negligent gesture that pulled his shirt against his broad shoulders. "I'll want to hash out some details."

"I'm free this evening." Having waited so long, she wanted to settle whatever last reservations he might have.

"Sorry. As it happens, I've got somewhere else I have to be tonight."

The phone had been ringing when he'd come in from his run and although Sloan would like nothing more than to resolve the details of his working agreement with Blythe, some things—and some people—could not be ignored.

Now that he'd bitten at the bait she'd dangled in front of him, Blythe was not about to let Sloan off the hook.

"How about lunch in my motor home on the set tomorrow? Around noon?"

"Lunch sounds great." He flashed a grin she had no doubt charmed the opposite sex from eight to eighty. Acknowledging Walter Stern for the first time, he said, "Hello, Walter. It's been a long time."

His tone was brusque, lacking in the warmth he'd bestowed on Blythe. She had the impression that Sloan wouldn't really mind if a great deal more time elapsed before they worked together again.

"Wyndham." The studio head's face was stony. His tone was no more cordial than Sloan's. There were currents there, Blythe considered. Currents she couldn't quite grasp.

Before she could get a handle on the tension between the two men, the trio was interrupted by the arrival of an aging actress literally dripping in diamonds.

"Walter!" The actress bestowed air kisses on each cheek. "I simply must talk to you about a project I have in mind." She glanced at Blythe dismissingly. "Hello, Blythe, darling," she cooed. "You wouldn't mind if I steal Walter away, would you?"

"Be my guest." Once they were alone, Blythe turned to Sloan. "I don't suppose you'd care to have our discussion now?"

As interested as he was in Blythe's film, Sloan had another, more personal project in mind. "I don't want to risk being interrupted," he said. "How about we just stay with tomorrow?"

Once again, it wasn't her first choice. Once again, Blythe realized she had scant choice. Like it or not, at this point Sloan—and, dammit, Walter Stern—were calling the shots.

"Tomorrow it is." Flashing him a smile that revealed not an iota of frustration, she drifted off in search of their hostess.

At the opposite end of the garden, still focused on what the fugitive squad could possibly want with her, Cait was engaged in thoughts of chasing a beleaguered, handsome Harrison Ford across the country when an all too familiar voice shattered the fantasy.

"Good afternoon, Officer."

She slowly turned around and found herself face-to-face with the man she'd been trying to forget ever since that debacle at Blythe's gate.

"I didn't realize you'd be here." Her tone was not welcoming.

"Don't you read *Variety?*" Sloan smiled charmingly, undeterred by her display of bad manners. He'd been watching her, aware of her discomfort and admiring the way she'd managed to conceal it so well. He'd also noticed she was distracted and wondered why. "I'm currently on all the *A* lists in town."

"Congratulations." Her dry tone said otherwise.

His brown eyes lit with humor. "Actually, I think it's more a case of be careful what you wish for. But," he shrugged his shoulders, "since it gets me first look at terrific projects like Blythe's, I'm in no position to complain."

He smiled again, but this time it was a slow, seductive smile she couldn't help imagining up on the silver screen. The smile slowly faded as he subjected her to a long silent study.

Refusing to let him know she was even the least bit affected, Cait stood absolutely still and let him look.

Her dress, Sloan considered, was about as far away from a stark blue police uniform as possible. Outrageously romantic, it could have washed off an Impressionist painting.

Soft drifts of pastel flowers adorned a full, tea-length skirt that he imagined would rustle when she walked. Her hair had been pulled back with a gold filigree clip and allowed to tumble down her back in a riot of fiery waves.

He'd spent the past four nights and much of this morning assuring himself that the spitfire in the hooker dress who'd waved that 9mm pistol in his face couldn't possibly be as lovely as he'd first thought.

Now, in the unforgiving light of bright, midday California sunshine, he realized that he'd only been partly right. Cait Carrigan wasn't as lovely as he'd remembered. She was, incredibly, even more so.

"You are," he said slowly, "the most beautiful woman I've ever seen."

The compliment, which she'd heard before, should not have made her heart beat faster. It should not, Cait told herself firmly. But it did.

"You disappoint me, Mr. Wyndham." She tapped an unpolished fingernail against her champagne glass and reminded herself to breathe. "I would have thought a man of your reputed talent would be able to come up with something a bit less clichéd."

"You'd think so, wouldn't you?" He smiled absently and wondered how it was that the pretty words of flattery that usually came trippingly off his tongue had deserted him.

Although Cait would fling herself off the top of the Hollywood sign before admitting it, Sloan didn't look all that bad himself.

He was wearing cream linen trousers, an ivory Egyptian cotton shirt with the sleeves rolled up almost to the elbows and buttery soft loafers. If she'd been a casting director, she would have found him ideal for the role of The Great Gatsby. He looked rich and successful and outrageously attractive.

Sloan rocked back on his heels and continued to peruse her. "You need a hat."

"A hat?" She instinctively raised a hand to her hair.

"You look as if you should be pouring Earl Grey from a Royal Doulton teapot in some English country garden. All you need to complete the image is a wide-brimmed straw hat with a full-blown white rose stuck in its ribbon band."

Here were the clever words Cait would have expected from a man who made a very good living with words. Before she could come back with a snappy response, he'd lifted a hand to her hair.

"I take it back," he murmured, seemingly entranced by the strands he was sifting through his long fingers. Cait tried to ignore the tingle of response his seemingly innocent touch inspired.

"What?" Her breath caught as those tantalizing fingers grazed her neck.

"A hat would hide this magnificent hair. And although I've never claimed to be the slightest bit religious, even I know that—" he lifted a thick swathe and inhaled "—would undoubtedly be a cardinal sin."

He annoyed her. Fascinated her. And worst of all, Sloan Wyndham frightened her in ways Cait couldn't begin to understand.

"Mr. Wyndham—"

"Sloan." He trailed his fingertips down the satin flesh of her throat and felt her pulse leap. "I'm not much on formality."

"Too bad." A puff of breeze caused a strand of hair to drift over her eyes. Frustrated, she blew it away. "Because I am. And if you don't take your hand off me right now, you're going to be sorry."

He grinned unrepentantly, but nevertheless did as she instructed. "Are you threatening me with police brutality, Officer?"

"I'm only telling you that you might be accustomed to women throwing themselves at your feet, but I'm not most women."

"Now that I've figured out for myself." Because he wanted to touch her again, he slipped his hands in his pockets and continued to look at her.

As she stared back at him, unwillingly transfixed, Cait vaguely heard a familiar voice call out her name. Glancing over toward the rock garden, Cait saw her mother headed toward them, like a sleek racing yacht at full sail.

"Cait, dear." Natalie touched a powdered and perfumed cheek against her daughter's. Her face, thanks to a secret, ridiculously expensive Swiss complexion formula and a recent facelift and chemical peel, looked at least a decade younger than her years. "I'm so pleased to see you." She turned to Sloan. "I see you've met my daughter, Sloan darling."

Darling? Cait's eyes narrowed as she watched her mother's hand settle on his arm. Diamonds from past failed marriages glittered like ice on three of her graceful, manicured fingers.

Although Cait had been telling herself that she didn't even like Sloan Wyndham, a sharp, green shaft of jealousy struck with the accuracy of an arrow hitting a bull's-eye right in the tender center of her heart.

Cait would have had to have been living these past years on Venus not to have heard about Sloan's reputed womanizing tendencies. But her mother?

"Actually, Cait and I met the other day," Sloan answered. Now that he realized LA's most gorgeous cop was actually Natalie Landis's daughter, he could see the resemblance.

Mother and daughter shared the same expressive emerald eyes and remarkably flawless complexion. Natalie's hair, worn today in a sleek French roll—all the better to display her chiseled cheekbones—was the color of winter wheat. Cait's unruly waves reminded him of the wildfires that tore through these hills during the dry season.

Natalie's body, while kept firm by daily visits from a personal trainer, was far lusher than her daughter's, but having always been a leg man himself, Sloan personally preferred Cait's long, coltish curves.

"I never realized you had a grown daughter," Sloan told the actress. "You could be sisters."

It was not false Hollywood flattery. It was pretty much the truth. Natalie Landis hadn't stopped the passage of time, but if her still stunning looks were any indication, she had managed to slow it to a crawl.

Natalie laughed, the musical, silvery bell sound designed to please a man's ear. "I was a child bride."

"Obviously you were still in your cradle," he agreed without missing a beat.

"That's what I adore about you, Sloan, darling." Her glossy lips curved in a pleased, intimate smile. "You always say precisely the right things."

She turned back to Cait. "You certainly look lovely today, dear. Doesn't she, Sloan?"

"Exquisite." His words were directed at Natalie, but his eyes were on Cait's face. And Lord, what a face it was, Sloan thought. "I'm amazed LAPD doesn't have every male in town drag racing down all the major streets, hoping to get pulled over by Officer Carrigan."

"Oh, please." Natalie groaned dramatically. "It's been such a lovely day. Let's not ruin it by discussing Cait's little rebellion."

Cait could not—would not—allow her mother's blatantly dismissive remark to go unchallenged. She raised her chin.

"It's not a *little* rebellion, mother. It's my career."

"So you keep telling me," Natalie agreed with a sigh. The deep breath caused her still remarkable breasts, clad in a thin, above-the-knee sheath of ivory silk, to rise and fall attractively. "Honestly, anyone would think you'd grown up in the Valley." She turned toward Sloan.

"Tell, me, darling," she practically crooned as her fingers stroked his arm, "were you a rebellious child?"

He almost laughed. The irony was too perfect. Sloan wondered how Natalie would respond if he assured her that he'd definitely been the least rebellious member of his infamous family.

"I think all kids need to find their own way, Nat." He gently, discreetly, took his arm away, a gesture that was not missed by Cait's sharp eyes.

"I suppose you're right," the older woman agreed with another sigh. "You usually are."

"I hadn't realized you two knew one another," Cait said.

"I know everyone," Natalie reminded her daughter sharply. Her tone immediately softened. "As a matter of fact, I've been trying to talk Sloan into working on a project with me." The famous voice turned signature sultry. "I think we'd make a simply marvelous team."

Cait shot him a sharp look; Sloan returned it with a bland one of his own. "Well, as delightful as this has been," Cait said, "I really do need to leave." That much was the truth. Another few minutes of watching her mother blatantly flirt with a man nearly half her age had Cait in danger of suffocating.

"Oh, you can't leave before the fashion show!" Natalie protested. She turned to Sloan. "It's going to be so absolutely precious. Karen—the volunteer from the Humane Society—has brought all these darling little dogs and kittens up from the animal shelter. We're dressing them up like characters from famous movies."

"Sounds cute." Sloan was beginning to understand Cait's discomfort.

"Adorable," Cait agreed dryly. "But I'm due at work soon."

"But I thought you had the day off."

"I thought I did, too. But I got a call transferred here a little while ago. They want me to come in to headquarters."

"I do so hate that horrid place," Natalie complained.

"So you've said." Cait glanced around, in search of Blythe.

"Looking for someone?" Sloan asked.

"Just Blythe. We came together." Cait saw her friend deep in conversation once again with Walter Stern III by the pool. Although both had their public faces on, she could tell they were arguing.

"I was just leaving," Sloan said. "Why don't I give you a lift?"

"Oh, you can't leave yet!" Natalie protested. "I was going to ask you to present the Norma Desmond award."

"Gee, Nat," Sloan apologized, "I'm truly honored. But I have to visit a sick friend."

"Really, Sloan." A lifetime of practice allowed Natalie to somehow frown without causing a single line in her smooth forehead. "If you don't wish to take part in the contest, just say so. But to tell such a blatant lie—"

"It's not a lie." He flashed her an appealingly boyish grin. "I really am sorry, but I only planned to drop by, say hello and give you my contribution." He pulled a check out of his shirt pocket.

Emerald green eyes widened. "Gracious. This is quite generous."

"It's only money. And it's for a good cause." He took hold of Natalie's hand and lifted her rose-tinted fingertips to his lips. "Nat, it's been delightful seeing you again. I'll give you a call next week. We'll have lunch and discuss a proposal I have for you."

To Cait's amazement and chagrin, her mother beamed like a starstruck fourteen-year-old when meeting her favorite rock idol. "Anytime," she agreed breathlessly.

Seeming not to notice the effect he'd had on the forty-something actress, Sloan turned toward Cait. "Ready to go?"

"I told you, I already have a ride."

"Blythe won't mind if you change your plans. Besides, I'd like a chance to prove to you that there are no hard feelings after our encounter the other day."

"Encounter?" Natalie pounced on his words like a sleek Siamese cat attacking a plump mouse.

"It's a long story," Sloan said quickly. Beside him he could feel Cait reaching the boiling point and considered that perhaps he'd pushed his luck. "And we really do have to go. Don't we, Cait?"

She wanted to inform him that she'd rather get into a car with Attila the Hun. But Cait also knew that if she remained here, she'd be subjecting herself to her mother's third degree. And in her own way, Natalie Landis could be every bit as unrelenting as the toughest downtown homicide cop.

"You need to tell Blythe I'm driving you home," he said. "And I need to talk with her about something."

"You are not driving me home," Cait continued to argue even as she allowed him to lead her away with a broad palm against her back. One thing she did not want to do was create a scene that would draw attention to them.

"Don't be such a hard-ass." Although his smile didn't flicker, Cait didn't miss the brief flare of irritation in his eyes.

She was forestalled from further argument when they reached Blythe, who'd just finished yet another frustrating conversation with Walter Stern.

"If I didn't know better, I'd think he was stonewalling," she said to Cait and Sloan, after revealing the gist of her encounter with the studio head. "It may just be that he wants to keep me in those horrid woman-in-jeopardy films, but whatever the reason, he's proving horribly uncooperative."

"How about hiring someone who knows how to uncover old secrets," Sloan suggested.

"Like a private detective?"

"Exactly."

Blythe turned toward Cait. "Do you know anyone?"

"You're in luck." Cait reached into her purse and pulled out one of the business cards she was never without these days and handed it to Blythe.

"Gage Remington?"

"My ex-partner on the force," Cait said. "Gage taught me everything I know about the street side of being a cop. He's gone into business for himself these days."

"There's no office address."

"He doesn't exactly have one. He lives on a boat in Marina del Rey, which he uses as a base of operations."

Despite Cait's recommendation, Blythe thought that Gage Remington sounded a bit too unconventional for her purposes.

"Give Gage a call," Cait urged, sensing her friend's hesitation. "He might not be the kind of stuffy, button-down guys you seem to prefer these days, but he's definitely one of the good guys."

Blythe glanced over at Sloan.

"If Cait is willing to vouch for him, I think we ought to give the guy a try."

Cait ground her teeth as he slanted her a smile that was both charming and effective.

"I suppose it won't hurt to talk to the man," Blythe decided. She slipped the card into her own purse.

"Why don't you give him a call now?" Sloan suggested. "So we'll know where we stand."

"You can call from the library," Cait volunteered, eager to help Gage's business take off. "He's been out of town. But he was due back this morning. If you're quick, you might be able to hire him before he takes on another case."

As luck would have it, Gage Remington agreed to meet with Blythe within the hour. Which, since Marina del Rey was in the opposite direction from Bel Air, effectively precluded Blythe driving Cait home before her meeting.

"Let me know how things go," Sloan said. "Meanwhile, Cait and I have places to go. People to see." Taking hold of Blythe's shoulders, he bent his head to kiss her cheek. "It's going to be fun working together, Blythe. I have a feeling we're going to make one helluva team."

The kiss was a friendly one with no sexual overtones. Blythe smiled up at him. "I'm looking forward to it."

"I suppose you think you're clever," Cait huffed as they waited for the valet to bring Sloan's Porsche around.

"Clever?"

The car arrived. When the valet—another gorgeous, obvious Hollywood wanna-be—opened the door, Cait settled into the passenger seat with a swirl of flowered skirt. "Manipulating me this way."

Sloan didn't answer until he was behind the wheel and had driven halfway down the long, curving redbrick driveway. "Not clever, merely desperate."

"Desperate?" Icicles of disbelief dripped from her tone. She couldn't imagine this man desperate. Sloan Wyndham was the most arrogant, self-assured male she'd ever met. And in this town, that was really saying something!

Frustrated from four long nights spent dreaming about this woman, and five equally long days fantasizing about her, Sloan pulled over to the side of the driveway and cut the engine.

"Desperate," he repeated. "Do you have any idea how much I've been wanting to do this?"

Before she could perceive his intention, before she could make the slightest move to stop him, Sloan pulled Cait into his arms.

5

FOR A LONG SUSPENDED moment, Cait stared up at him, a hundred—a thousand—feelings battering away inside her, fighting for control. Her breath caught, then shuddered out as she watched. And waited.

He took her mouth with the easy confidence of a man who'd kissed more women than he could count. He didn't rush. His lips somehow managed to be firm and soft at the same time. They plucked at hers, tasting at their leisure, lingering, trapping her in gauzy layers of sensation.

Cait was twenty-five years old. She'd certainly been kissed before, beginning with the time Johnny Matthews had cornered her in the history section of the school library, although she wasn't certain that counted because she'd slugged him in the jaw, causing him to bang the back of his head against the shelf.

By the time he'd come to, sneaky little Kristy Longview, who'd been watching the aborted kiss, had called the teacher, who'd called the principal, who sentenced both Cait and her would-be lothario to a week of erasing chalk boards after school.

The Matthews—Mr. Matthew being an attorney— threatened to sue, but Cait's father, no lightweight himself at making threats, had pointed out the ridicule that would be heaped on the eleven-year-old boy if it became public knowledge that he'd been KO'd by a mere girl.

After that less than auspicious introduction to romance, other boys had followed in Johnny's wake, and although

Cait had welcomed their kisses with varying degrees of enthusiasm, none—not one in all the intervening years—had ever caused her mind to empty. Until Sloan.

She should stop him, Cait told herself.

She would stop him, she promised herself.

Soon.

With his mouth on hers, coherent thought vanished, disappearing into the soft silvery mists clouding her mind.

His hands were wandering through her hair as if they had every right to be there. Restrained passion flared in the dark whiskey depths of his eyes. Fascinated and a little frightened, she wanted to keep her eyes open, but when his teeth began nibbling at the soft flesh at the inside of her bottom lip, Cait's lids drifted shut on a soft, shimmering sigh.

Sweet. He never would have suspected that Officer Cait Carrigan could be so impossibly sweet. Tasting her was like dining on honeyed nectar. He ran his hand down the side of her face and discovered that touching her was like touching warm satin.

Sloan wanted to taste her all over.

He wanted to touch her everywhere.

He wanted her. In every way possible. And a few they'd discover for themselves.

Against every vestige of common sense she possessed, Cait wanted to thrust her hands into the shaggy chestnut waves skimming his collar, but just in time, some last little vestige of reason remaining in the back of her mind counseled restraint.

Instead, she forced herself to be satisfied with holding on to the tops of his arms. He was as hard and muscular as he'd looked when she'd first spotted him up on that gate. The difference was he was proving to be far more dangerous than she'd first thought.

Seductive images swam giddily through her mind. Lush, erotic images that made her blood hum and her body ache. When his tongue traced a slow, lazy circle around her parted lips, she experienced a rush of need so strong that if she'd not already been sitting down she would have gone weak in the knees.

On the heels of that jolt came another realization every bit as unexpected. And as painful. She was, Cait realized through her swimming senses, afraid.

Never had one man brought her to such a precipice with a single kiss.

And never had she experienced such an ominous feeling of fear from any man.

He was drawing out every ounce of her will with his mouth alone. Without taking his hands from her hair, he was causing her entire body to quiver.

Because she knew this was getting too dangerous, too fast, Cait managed, with effort, to open her eyes. Realizing that her fingers were splayed against the front of his shirt—how on earth did they get there?—she pushed against his chest.

"No."

His only response was a muffled groan as his lips continued their deep sensual torment. Suddenly aware of exactly how close she'd come to losing all control—in her mother's driveway, for Pete's sake!—Cait shoved again. Harder.

"Dammit, I said no!"

Sloan couldn't think. His heart was pounding like a runaway freight train and if she'd held her pistol to his head and told him to get out of the car right now, he would not have been able to move. But that single word, spoken with such resolve, and amazingly, fear, struck home.

Reluctantly, he released her mouth. Choking back a frustrated curse, he lowered his hands.

Cait assured herself that the only reason she'd reacted so uncharacteristically to Sloan's kiss was that he'd caught her totally by surprise.

But even as she tried to make herself believe that, she secretly admitted it was a lie. Unwilling to allow Sloan to know that he possessed such power over her, she folded her arms across her chest and glared at him.

"Is that how you kiss my mother?"

He could still taste her. A man who refused to apologize for his appetites—whether it came to good food, fine brandy, fast cars, or beautiful, willing women—Sloan knew that one taste of Cait Carrigan would never be enough.

She was more than he'd dreamed. And, as impossible as it seemed, she was turning out to be even more than he'd fantasized.

Although self-restraint had never been his long suit, Sloan could, when absolutely necessary, be patient. Telling himself that there would be a next time, and soon, he managed a slow, lazy smile.

"A gentleman doesn't kiss and tell."

His easy arrogance annoyed her. As did his obscure answer. "She's old enough to be your mother."

He shrugged, once again drawing her unwilling attention to his broad shoulders. "Actually, she's not. But it doesn't matter. Because if I wanted your mother, Cait, I certainly wouldn't let any difference in our ages stand in my way."

That she believed. Cait doubted this man let anything stand in the way of anything—or anyone—he wanted.

Sloan laughed, a rich, deep sound that vibrated through her even as she tried to remain annoyed. "Anyone ever tell you that you're gorgeous when you're jealous, Cait?"

"I'm not jealous." Her voice was a sheet of ice.

"Whatever you say. But for the record, you don't have to worry about me becoming your next stepfather."

"Are you saying you're not interested in my mother?"

"Of course I'm interested. I'm interested in Natalie as a friend. I'm also interested in her professionally as a surprisingly good, remarkably bankable actor."

A wicked light gleamed in his eyes, a sexy smile claimed his lips. He ran the backs of his fingers in a slow, tantalizing sweep up her cheekbone.

"I also happen to be very interested in Natalie's very delectable daughter. In the most personal way possible."

His low husky voice slipped beneath her still warm skin, causing every one of her nerve endings to sizzle.

"What's the matter," Cait snapped, annoyed by the dizzying way he was making her feel, "am I the only female below the age of sixty in this town you haven't lured into your bed?"

Rather than take offense at her words, as she'd intended, he had the gall to appear amused. "There are one or two others who have escaped my attention."

Cait folded her arms. "Imagine that."

"Believe it or not," he said mildly, as he twisted the key in the ignition, causing the Porsche to come to life with a throaty purr, "I've progressed beyond thinking with my glands."

"You've no idea how that relieves me."

The lady was definitely no cream puff. Fortunately, Sloan had always enjoyed a challenge. He threw back his head and laughed.

"Private joke?" she asked stiffly, wondering if he was actually laughing at her.

He shook his head and his eyes, as they slid her way, were lit with a mixture of mirth and resignation.

"In a way."

"I see." Actually, she didn't understand anything about Sloan, or even about herself whenever she was around him, but Cait was damned if she'd admit that.

"Ah, sweet Cait, if you only knew how ironic this all is." Buck Riley's kid falling for a cop.

Hell, Sloan figured his father must be spinning in his grave right about now.

As for his mother . . .

His slight, unconscious sigh stopped Cait's planned sarcastic response cold. For a fleeting second, she saw the self-assured mask slip and viewed something that looked remarkably like pain move across his handsome features. Against her will, something unbidden and entirely unwelcome stirred deep in her heart.

Instead she concentrated on directions. In order to cut her commute time down, Cait had recently moved from her funky Venice bungalow to an apartment in the Wilshire district. Following her instructions, Sloan had no trouble finding the building.

"Nice place," he said admiringly as he pulled up in front of the apartment house which had been painted in a soft Mediterranean pink.

"I like it."

"I can see why. There are too few buildings with a past anymore in this town. The city fathers seem to have a compulsion to tear down anything even moderately historical and replace it with a parking lot. Or a mall."

Although she hated discovering that there was something she shared in common with this man, Cait felt exactly the same way.

It was bad enough that the ice-cream shop across Sunset Boulevard from Hollywood High where Lana Turner had been discovered sipping a soda—despite persistent stories of the glamorous actress being discovered at Schwab's—

was now a minimall. And Cait considered the famous, original "Hat" Brown Derby being turned into part of another shopping center nothing short of heresy.

Without waiting for the argument he knew would be forthcoming, Sloan was out of the car, intending to open the passenger door. He was not all that surprised when Cait opened her own door and was on the sidewalk before he could get around the front of the Porsche.

"Well, thanks for the lift," she said breezily. "But I really do have to run."

"I'll walk you to your door."

"Really, that's not necessary."

"Not only does a gentleman never kiss and tell, he always sees a lady home."

He'd put his arm around her shoulder in a gesture that Cait found decidedly possessive. When she went to shrug off the light touch, his fingers tightened.

Not wanting to waste time, or draw attention by standing here arguing on the sidewalk, Cait decided to give him this one.

"Is that something you learned from your mother?" she asked.

"No." A plaque on the outside wall by the arched front doorway read Bachelor Arms. Below the plaque, someone had scratched Believe the legend. "It's not."

His tone was gruff. His handsome face had closed up. But that strange pain she'd viewed earlier was back. The idea that he might possibly have hidden depths only made him more dangerous.

Her apartment was on the third floor. Neither spoke as they climbed the stairs. "This is it," she said, stopping in front of 3-C. She turned away and slipped the key into the dead bolt lock. "Well, thanks for the ride."

Unwilling to let her get away quite so soon, Sloan took hold of her arm and turned her back toward him.

Cait opened her mouth to complain about being man-handled. But the intriguing, soft-focus look in his whiskey brown eyes stopped the words in her throat.

"What would you say," he asked on a husky tone that made her pulse jump, "if I asked if I could kiss you again?"

He leaned down, his face a whisper away from hers. He was close. Too close.

She put her hand against the front of his shirt, intending to push him away. "I'd say no."

He covered her hand with his larger, darker one. His other arm wrapped around her waist, hauling her against him until their bodies were touching, chest-to-chest, thigh-to-thigh.

She thought of all the reasons why she didn't want him to touch her. All the reasons why she couldn't allow him to kiss her.

And then, as his mouth captured hers, Cait couldn't think at all.

Unlike the first time, where Sloan had led her slowly, tantalizingly into the mists, the power of this kiss slammed into her. She was swept breathless into a raging storm. Thunder roared in her ears, lightning flashed behind her closed eyes. Her body quaked.

There was no cool control here. No clever seduction. His mouth was hot and open and urgent, his tongue a weapon, diving deeper and deeper, not only to taste, but to torment.

Rather than pushing him away, her arms wrapped around his waist. She strained against him, seeking to ease the dark ache building inside her.

Sloan felt himself being sucked into the whirlwind. He felt the power, the strength, the madness. Her lips softened, but did not yield. Her body pressed against his, demanding, but not surrendering.

He wanted as he'd never wanted before. Needed as he'd never needed. Although Sloan's reputation was not as nearly tarnished as the supermarket rags liked to suggest, it was true he'd known more than his share of women. But never had he met one who matched his needs so perfectly.

Sloan wanted, with a desperation that went all the way to the bone, to kick down her door and drag her inside her apartment where he'd spend the rest of the day and night ravishing every inch of her delectable, fragrant body. But because he understood, from that tense exchange with her mother, exactly how important Cait's career was to her, he knew that it would have to wait.

And there would definitely be, he vowed, as he felt her soft, silk-clad breasts melding against his rigid chest, another time. Hundreds of them.

With a very real regret, and ignoring her faint, murmured protest, he lifted his head. He retrieved her hands, which were threatening to scorch the back of his shirt, and lifted them to his lips.

It had happened again! A primitive beat sang in her blood as Cait blinked in a desperate attempt to clear her whirling mind.

Sloan could see her pulse still pounding in her throat, and the passion still swirling in her remarkable green eyes. *Soon*, he promised himself.

"You didn't say no," Sloan reminded her.

Cait was grateful for the return of his easy male arrogance. This, she told herself, she could handle. "I didn't say yes," she reminded him.

Her voice, miraculously, managed to sound reasonably strong and confident, belying the truth that her knees were trembling. It was going to be all right. She was going to be all right. At least that's what Cait told herself.

But then Sloan smiled.

And her heart stopped.

"Yes, you did," he answered on that husky voice that had such a devastating way of slipping beneath her already heated flesh.

Before she could argue, he surprised her by flicking a casual finger down her nose. "You'd better go in," he suggested. "You don't want to be late."

He gave her another smile, even more devastating than any of the others. And then he turned and went back down the stairs, taking them two at a time. By the time he'd reached the first landing, Cait could hear him whistling.

Irritated at him for arousing her, furious at herself for being aroused, Cait slammed into her apartment, marched into the bedroom and yanked her uniform off its hanger.

Outside on the street, Sloan's mind was still filled with Cait. Sweet, soft Cait who smelled like a gypsy's cache of magical spices and tasted like heaven.

As he climbed back into the Porsche, he did not notice one of the tenants cutting flowers from the beds in front of the three-story apartment building.

The elderly woman had watched the pair's arrival. A veteran of the romance wars herself, Natasha Kuryan could certainly recognize passion when she saw it.

The former beauty and onetime makeup artist to the stars smiled. Things around Bachelor Arms were about to get interesting.

FAMOUS AS THE WORLD'S largest man-made small craft harbor, home to seafaring vessels from Hobie Cat sailboats to sloops, Marina del Rey was a little over a mile square in area, half of which was water. Less noisy and far less crowded than most of Los Angeles, the small community boasted four parks, numerous bicycle and jogging paths and a replica of an old New England fishing town that featured jazz on Sunday afternoons.

The mood throughout the compact seaside village was relaxed. Casual. Which worried Blythe as she circled the harbor on Admiralty Way. If Cait's detective was as laid-back as she suspected, he wasn't the man she was looking for.

She'd already attempted to unearth information about Alexandra Romanov, only to find herself stymied at every turn. And apparently, Sloan Wyndham had no more luck, or he wouldn't have suggested hiring a detective in the first place.

No, she decided as she turned off Via Marina onto Bora Bora Way, she didn't need to hire some easygoing Jim Rockford or Thomas Magnum clone; the private investigator she was seeking would have to be not only sharp as a tack, he'd also have to be a go-getter. And although Marina del Rey was, admittedly, one of the prettier areas in the county, she couldn't imagine anyone with any real motivation living here.

She followed his instructions, finding the slip without difficulty. The sloop bobbing gently at the deck was sleek and white. And expensive. Perhaps she'd misjudged Gage Remington, Blythe considered.

Then again, perhaps not.

As she climbed out of her racing green Jaguar and approached the sloop, she caught sight of the man sitting in a canvas chair on the deck. He was wearing a white polo shirt and blue shorts and seemed engrossed in a tout sheet from Hollywood Park.

Although she'd spent most of her life in the high-stakes world of movie making, Blythe was not overly fond of gamblers.

Her high heels tapped on the wooden dock. Hearing the sound, Gage put the racing form down and pushed himself out of the yellow canvas chair with a lazy grace.

It was all Gage could do not to groan as he watched Blythe Fielding walking toward him in the brisk, long-legged stride of a woman accustomed to getting her way.

Actresses had never been one of his favorite people. There had been times, during his days working in the cop shop, when he'd been assigned to baby-sit some hotshot movie or television star who was researching a role. As a rule, he'd found them not very bright, entirely self-absorbed and unwilling even to try to understand what the job was about.

They came to the station, their beautiful heads filled with images born in the minds of scriptwriters, expecting daily hostage situations, homicides and shoot-outs in the downtown streets.

They expected cops to be some impossible hybrid of Clint Eastwood, Mel Gibson and Angie Dickinson, and when he unsurprisingly failed to pull off such lofty expectations, they invariably went away disappointed and ended up playing whatever role they'd been researching the same inaccurate, shoot-'em-up way it had been done countless times before.

His first impression of the woman walking toward him on those impractical high heel sandals and wearing that flowing white silk dress that looked more suitable to some Beverly Hills garden party than hanging around on a boat was that she was no different from the others.

Her dark hair had been piled atop her head in some artfully casual style he suspected had taken some chichi Rodeo Drive hairdresser hours to arrange. It gleamed like jet in the slanting afternoon sun. The designer sunglasses she was wearing kept him from seeing her eyes, but he'd seen enough of Blythe Fielding's movies to know that they were wide and dark and thickly lashed.

"Mr. Remington?" Her voice was every bit as lush and rich as it sounded in all those darkened theaters. Even as he felt himself responding to those full seductive tones, it crossed Gage's mind that he also detected a taut note of disapproval.

He pulled off his own sunglasses. "That's me." He gave her a faint, welcoming smile he was a very long way from feeling. Working on an undercover thoroughbred doping sting, he was due at the racetrack in an hour; she was already ten minutes late.

His eyes were a blue so pale as to appear almost silver. A startling contrast to his black hair and deeply tanned skin, they were also looking at her as if he wished she'd driven into the harbor on her way to the slip.

Normally irritated by the way most men tended to view her as just another pretty face or sexy body, Blythe was surprised to find exactly how disconcerting she was finding his obvious disapproval.

Not one to reveal personal feelings, especially any insecurities she might be harboring, Blythe held out a polite hand. "I'm Blythe Fielding."

As if it would be necessary for her to introduce herself to any male on the planet. Not only had Gage recognized her name the moment he'd heard it on the phone, he'd also seen enough of her films to know exactly what her lush body looked like beneath that white dress.

She was standing there, waiting expectantly. Having no other choice, Gage extended his own hand. "I know who you are, Ms. Fielding." His fingers curled around hers. Her palm was soft, her grip surprisingly firm.

"I'm sorry I'm late. But the traffic was horrendous for a Sunday."

"No problem," he lied. "Let me help you aboard."

His wide palm was ridged with calluses. "Thank you, but that's really not necessary."

His gaze skimmed over her slender ankles, rounded calves and firm thighs, nicely curved hips and *Sports Illustrated* cover girl breasts on a lazy journey to her face. "You're not exactly dressed for climbing aboard boats, Ms. Fielding."

This time she couldn't miss the censure in his voice. Blythe decided that there was absolutely no way on God's green earth she was going to hire this man. "I told you I was calling from another engagement." She tugged her hand free.

"That you did." Not trusting those spindly little shoes, he put both his hands on her waist and lifted her from the floating dock onto the deck of the sleek sloop. "You just failed to mention you were having tea with the Queen."

His long dark fingers had claimed possession as if they had every right to be wrapped around her waist.

"Not the Queen," she corrected with a toss of the head that had him waiting for her hair to come tumbling down. He was vaguely disappointed when it stayed in place. "Natalie Landis."

Cait's glamorous, larger-than-life mother. Gage knew Natalie well, liked her immensely, found her bright and sexy and amusing, and still understood exactly why Cait often felt like a changeling. "Same thing," he said.

His voice had a lazy slow drawl that, while no Texas twang, bespoke western roots. They were standing close enough together that she had to tilt her head back to look up at him.

"You're not exactly what I expected."

Neither was he the man she'd been hoping for. Although she couldn't deny Gage Remington was sexy, in a tousled, outdoor kind of way, the fact that he'd chosen to dress in those brief cotton shorts and snug polo shirt and sneakers for a business consultation only underscored her worry that he wasn't the detective for her job.

"That's funny." The white silk felt smooth and soft beneath his fingertips. Gage knew, without the slightest doubt, that her fragrant skin would be smoother. And softer. "You're pretty much what I was expecting."

Blythe was already tired of his attitude. "Do you always insult prospective employers?" she asked in a cool ice-maiden tone that he recognized from her last film, where she'd played a female serial killer who had a nasty habit of knocking off rich old husbands.

"Only ones who have made their minds up about me before they get to know me."

His point. He might not be the intense, type *A* personality she'd been hoping to meet, but Gage Remington was turning out to be more perceptive than she'd first thought.

"I haven't made my mind up about anything," she said.

Especially coming from an actress, that was about the most unconvincing lie Gage had ever heard. And in his line of work, he'd heard some doozies.

Not certain whether he was amused or annoyed, Gage shrugged. "Whatever you say."

Blythe looked up into his unreadable face and wondered why Cait had neglected to mention that her former partner was sexier than any male had a right to be. She'd grown up in a town where gorgeous men—and women—were the norm. Not that Gage Remington was movie star gorgeous. Throw a stick on any beach along the Pacific Coast Highway and you'd hit a dozen men much better looking than this one. He was tall and rangy. Like a long distance runner, Blythe considered. Or better yet, a cowboy. His face was too harshly cut to be classically handsome, his steely blue eyes were too heavily hooded, and his nose appeared to have been broken on more than one occasion. His mouth wouldn't have been so bad, she considered, if it hadn't been set in such an ironic sneer.

But there was something about him—something deep and dark and potentially dangerous—that she unwillingly found fascinating.

She'd never met anyone remotely like him in the rarified circles in which she'd always lived and worked and played. Blythe had the feeling she never would.

Whatever else he was, Gage Remington was one of a kind.

His touch was outwardly casual, but the intent she felt radiating from him was unnervingly intimate. His vivid blue eyes—eyes that drew you in, deeper and deeper, until you had the feeling every secret you possessed was revealed—were riveted on her face, looking at Blythe so hard and so deep that she was grateful for the dark lenses that kept him from reading her suddenly tumultuous thoughts.

"You don't have to hold on to me any longer."

Her fragrance, every bit as dark and sultry as those drop-dead gorgeous eyes he knew were hiding behind those oversize lenses was the kind that sneaked up on a man, hitting him between the eyes—and more painfully, between the legs—when he least expected it.

Gage reminded himself that Hollywood was a town built on images and illusions and the illusion Blythe Fielding projected up on that silver screen was undoubtedly as false as the melted yellow grease theaters poured over popcorn and insisted on calling butter.

But even knowing that didn't make the assault on his senses any less devastating. "I like holding on to you."

She felt the tremor slide up her spine, then down. This was ridiculous. She was accustomed to setting the tone and pace of her business meetings.

Blythe had always prided herself on her control. And her restraint, which was a direct contrast to her steamy screen image. Despite whatever he might think of her, she was definitely not the type of woman to allow a complete stranger to touch her so familiarly.

She backed away. Gage released her, letting her break the light contact without comment.

"Why don't you sit down," he suggested, "and we can discuss how I'm going to find the facts surrounding your murdered Russian movie star."

Blythe turned her choices over in her mind. Pride prevented her from leaving, while a very strong stubborn streak kept her from giving up on her quest to discover the truth about Alexandra Romanov's death.

Reminding herself that Cait had recommended this man highly, and realizing that she had no idea how to go about finding a reputable detective among the myriad listings in the yellow pages, Blythe decided that she may as well go through with their meeting.

"I don't have much information," she warned as she sat down in the canvas chair he'd indicated with a wave of his dark hand.

"That's why you're hiring me."

"I hadn't realized we'd agreed on that." Having been caught off balance, Blythe was determined to regain control of this situation.

"You want the best, don't you?"

She lifted her chin. "Of course."

A flash of tanned thigh as she crossed those long legs caught his attention, making Gage think that perhaps there might just be some perks to this case, after all.

"Well, I'm the best."

"Some people might call that arrogance, Mr. Remington."

"Probably would," he agreed lazily. "But it wouldn't change things. Like it or not, Ms. Fielding, I'm your man. If I decide to take your case."

"If *you* decide?"

He saw her stiffen. Her voice went up in a dangerous way that had Gage suspecting that this ice princess's hot screen image might not be so far off the mark. Having a temper himself, he could recognize the signs in others. He also found the heat in her tone undeniably arousing.

"One of the advantages of working for myself, instead of the cops, is only having to take on jobs that interest me," he explained. "I'll admit to being mildly intrigued with the brief story you told me on the phone." He sat down across from her, stretched his long dark legs out in front of him, crossing them at the ankles. "So, since we're both busy people, we might as well get down to business.

"And let's start," he instructed in an uncompromising tone Blythe was not accustomed to hearing from anyone, "by taking off those damn glasses. I like to see who I'm doing business with."

Normally, she would have refused such a gruff, nononsense order. But angry at the way this former cop had her feeling so defensive, she ripped them off with a haughty gesture.

Blythe met Gage's steady, unblinking stare with a challenging look of her own.

And then it happened.

As impossible as it would later seem, when she had time to analyze the unnerving moment, Blythe heard the click

of something that strangely, impossibly, seemed like recognition.

A heartbeat later, her mind was wiped as clean as new
glass.

6

FROM THE OUTSIDE, the rambling white building set on the cliffs overlooking the vast blue Pacific Ocean could have been a resort hotel catering to the rich and famous. The lush lawns were a dark emerald green, bright flowers tumbled over the edges of the many brick planters, palm trees swayed gently in the soft sea breeze.

Guests strolled across those lawns, played tennis on the red clay courts and sat beneath the shade of flowering trees, reading, doing needlework, or just gazing out at the million-dollar view.

It was a sylvan scene that suggested wealth and privilege and comfort.

Only a closer study would reveal the wrought iron grill work barring all the windows, the electronic gates set in the high white walls and the guards stationed discreetly amidst the guests, who, in a less expensive facility would have been referred to as patients.

Sloan felt his heart clench as he flashed his visitor's pass to the guard at the gate. He hated coming here. He hated the smells of disinfectant and illness and despair that no amount of money could wash away. He hated the empty look in the eyes of the people who lived behind these white walls. And he hated the hopeless, helpless way the Safe Harbor Sanitarium made him feel.

Every time he drove through the gate, he told himself that this was the last time. That he just couldn't take it anymore. That she wouldn't even know if he never came again.

But Sloan could no more stop coming than he could stop breathing.

He parked his car in the assigned lot and handed his keys over to the attendant. Ever since a patient had stolen a set of Chrysler New Yorker car keys from a visiting grandfather and taken the police on a high speed, death-defying chase down the PCH, security had been tightened even more than usual.

The shift was changing. One of the doctors just coming off duty waved a cheery greeting. Sloan and the leggy blond psychiatrist whom he'd discovered harbored a secret passion for silk stockings, lace garter belts, and Victorian erotica had shared a brief, tempestuous fling a few years ago. As with most of the women Sloan had been involved with, they'd stayed friends.

"Hello, Sloan." Her full lips smiled; her eyes were filled with a sympathy he was not accustomed to seeing from the women he'd slept with. Then again, Sloan reminded himself grimly, Dr. Helen Taylor was the only woman who knew his painful secret.

"Hi, Helen." He tried to return her smile, but could only manage a crooked grimace. "How is she?"

"Better." This time the sympathy bordered on pity, making him remember why he'd broken off their relationship. "We adjusted her medication after that little episode the other day. She's been a great deal less agitated."

He straightened his shoulders. An iron fist curled round his gut. "Which means you've got her zoned out."

The doctor did not deny his accusation. "It's better than the alternative." Dr. Taylor lifted a palm to his cheek. "If you ever need to talk, or anything else..." Her voice drifted off, but not before Sloan heard the feminine invitation in her tone.

This time his smile was a bit more successful. But it still didn't reach his bleak, haunted eyes.

"Thanks. But I don't think that's such a good idea."

She sighed. "Of course, you're right. But I do so worry about you."

"Who, me?" he asked with feigned surprise.

"You need someone in your life, Sloan. It's not healthy for you to be alone like this."

"Why, Doc, don't you read the tabloids? I've got so many women in my hedonistic, bachelor's bed that every time a new one climbs in beneath the sheets, another one pops out on the other side."

She smiled, as she was supposed to. "Even if you were the libertine those horrid papers make you out to be, which you're not, we both know that having a lover is not necessarily the same as having someone to love."

"As it happens, I think I might have found someone."

"I'm glad." Her pleasure was not at all feigned, making him think, not for the first time in the past five years, how lucky he was to have this woman in his corner.

She went up on her toes and gave him a quick, friendly kiss. "Good luck."

Sloan didn't know if she was referring to Cait or today's visit. As he made his way across the rolling green lawn, he decided he could probably use a little luck in both cases.

He found her sitting all alone, on a concrete bench in the meditation garden. She was dressed in the white cotton caftan he'd brought her the last time he was here, the evening he'd almost gotten his head blown off climbing Blythe's fence. Full and loose, designed for comfort, the dress was adorned with white lace at the neckline, hems and sleeves.

He'd bought it while shooting on location in Cancun, hoping she'd enjoy it, even knowing that most of the time

simple emotions like joy and pleasure and sorrow were beyond her.

Her blond hair, which he could still remember being a
rich, gleaming honey, was streaked with gray. It hung lank
over her thin shoulders, reminding him that he should arrange to have it trimmed and shaped.

She was hugging a stuffed teddy bear that had been re-
paired too many times to count to her breast and was rock-
ing gently, back and forth, her amber eyes focused on some
distant scene from some long ago past that was constantly
replaying in her frail, damaged mind.

The pain proved suffocating. Sloan hitched in a deep
breath, and sat down beside her.

She turned, those once lovely eyes looking at him without the faintest shred of recognition.

Sloan took both her pale, slender hands in his.

Part of him felt seven years old again. Another part of him
felt older than time.

Although it took a herculean effort, he willed a smile onto
his face and into his eyes.

"Hiya, Mom."

ON THE RARE OCCASION Cait had ventured into L.A. police
headquarters in the past, the desk sergeant had barely ac-
knowledged her presence.

Today, however, things were decidedly different. Today,
the grizzled, balding veteran greeted her effusively. And as
he led her through the hallways lined with photos of past
police chiefs, back into the current chief's inner sanctum,
Cait had the impression that he was looking at her with a
strange mixture of envy and sympathy.

Although she'd arrived precisely on time, as the sergeant
ushered her into the conference room, she discovered not
only her own superiors, but representatives from several

other L.A. county police jurisdictions already seated around the large walnut table.

A quick glance revealed captains from Santa Monica, Venice, Redondo Beach, Manhattan Beach and Newport Beach as well as two deputies clad in the regulation khaki uniform of the L.A. Sheriff's department. In addition, she recognized the police commissioner, the mayor, and two grim-faced men whose blue suits, starched white shirts and black wing tips revealed them to be FBI agents.

"Good afternoon, Officer Carrigan," Captain Rodman, her own division superior greeted her.

Cait nodded, squelching the impulse to salute. "Sir." Her brisk, professional tone did not reveal either her sudden nervousness or her curiosity.

"Please. Have a seat." He gestured toward the single remaining vacant chair which just happened to be situated next to the commissioner. "Would you care for some coffee?"

The idea of a man of such superior rank offering her something to drink piqued Cait's curiosity even more.

"No, thank you, sir," she said, moving toward the chair he'd indicated. "I'm fine."

Every eye in the room watched as she sat down. Cait's spine remained as stiff as the starch in her uniform blouse. She could have been standing at attention.

Captain Rodman proceeded to introduce the others. Most of the names and some of the faces were familiar to her. All greeted her with professional politeness, although it crossed her mind that they seemed to be judging her. Worse yet, from the frown on some of the grimly set faces, she had the uneasy feeling that more than one of the assembled men were finding her lacking in some essential way.

"I imagine you're wondering why we've asked you here today."

"Yes, sir."

"It seems we have a problem." He folded his hands atop the table and gave her a long, level look. "And it occurred to me that you might be just the individual to assist us."

"I see," Cait said, not seeing anything at all.

At least, she considered with a cooling rush of relief, she hadn't been ordered here for a reprimand. When she'd first seen the mayor and commissioner, she'd worried that perhaps Sloan had filed a citizen's complaint against her, after all.

He paused to leaf through a manila folder. "You've been on the force four years?" he asked.

Although she realized since he was reading her file, the captain knew exactly how long she'd been a cop, Cait dutifully answered. "That's right. Four years, sir. And five months."

"Yes." He nodded and ran the side of his finger along his top lip, an unconscious gesture left over from when he'd sported a mustache. "I see you profess a desire to work in the Sex Crimes Unit."

Cait nodded yet again. "Yes, sir. Although I enjoy all aspects of police work, I feel I could be an asset in that area." She did not mention that having had a close friend who'd been raped in college, Cait felt she could bring a much needed empathy to the emotionally demanding work.

It was his turn to nod again. "Several of your superior officers appear to feel the same way. And your psychological testing scores are very encouraging."

"Thank you, sir." Cait was growing more curious and more impatient by the minute. Across the table, she saw the mayor begin to fidget. Obviously she was not the only one wishing Captain Rodman would just skip to the chase.

"The Vice detectives who have been working with you in the Hollywood division also say you're their best decoy. Your arrest and conviction rate is at the top of the squad."

"I've had very good training. And a great deal of help, sir."

She did not mention that although she'd found what had become known as The John Squad an interesting change from patrol car duty in the beginning, the challenge had begun to wear off. She was also needing weekly pedicures to soothe the blisters caused by pounding the pavement in high heels every day.

"Yes." He cleared his throat, rested his elbows on the walnut table and eyed her thoughtfully over his linked fingers. "We have a proposal for you, Officer Carrigan," he said. "One which you should think about carefully before you agree to accept."

He exchanged a brief look with the commissioner, who, with a curt nod, sent a silent message Cait could not understand.

"If you do choose to accept," he continued, making Cait feel as if she'd suddenly been zapped back in time to the set of "Mission Impossible," "and bring it to a satisfactory conclusion, I will personally recommend your promotion to the Sex Crimes Unit."

Cait still had no idea what the assignment he was referring to was. But it didn't matter.

Because she knew that if it would help her get the plum assignment that had been her goal since graduating from the Police Academy, she was definitely going to say yes.

THE DAY AFTER the Pet Parade Brunch, Natasha Kuryan stood in front of Bachelor Arms, awaiting the car that would take her to the Regent Beverly Wilshire, where, in the elegant, European-style Lobby Lounge, she and three long-time friends would have tea.

She knew younger moviegoers would undoubtedly recognize the hotel as the one where millionaire businessman Richard Gere ensconced himself with pretty woman Julia Roberts. High-style shoppers would think of it as the hotel that anchored south Rodeo Drive.

But Natasha would always remember the grand Beverly Hills hotel as the site where, in December of 1928, she spent a clandestine, glorious weekend with Gary Cooper, from the film *Wings*— Even now, decades later, memories of the charismatic actor's passionate, weakeningly slow love-making could still send a wicked heat coursing through her veins.

Natasha sighed. Youth, she thought, not for the first time, was definitely wasted on the young. What she wouldn't give for a chance to replay that weekend instead of her planned afternoon of eating scones and drinking tea and gossiping with a clutch of gabby old women.

A white stretch limo pulled up to the curb. A muscularly fit young man in a snug navy blue T-shirt, white jeans and running shoes climbed out of the driver's seat, greeted her with a dazzling flash of perfect white teeth and opened the limousine door with a dramatic flourish.

The hotel was not that far away; Natasha and her friends—a former studio hairdresser, a former costume designer and a one-time character actress—could easily have taken a taxi. But the four women were survivors of the old studio system.

They could remember when Hollywood was the most glamorous spot on earth. Unable to do anything about the passage of time and unable to bring back those glory days, they nevertheless insisted on maintaining some vestige of the old glamour. Which was why, on the first Monday of every month, they always traveled to tea in a long white limousine.

Natasha settled into the lush leather seat with a flourish of lacy peasant skirts. Busy greeting the others, she failed to see Blythe's Jaguar pull up in front of the apartment house.

As Blythe parked in front of Cait's sun-washed pink building, she had a sudden, unbidden feeling of déjà vu. "That's impossible," she murmured. "You've never been here." The strange feeling was followed by an even eerier one of foreboding.

"You really have been working too hard," she scolded herself as she shook off the unsettling emotions.

Although her lunch meeting with Sloan had gone surprisingly well—his enthusiasm had equaled hers and his demands had been few—it was more than a little apparent that they both had a great deal of work to do before bringing the film to production.

The building really was charming, Blythe considered as she walked up the brick walk. It boasted turquoise trim, lacy iron grillwork on the windows and balconies on the upper floors and a turret, which while not in keeping with its Spanish style, somehow seemed to fit.

"Bachelor Arms." She read the plaque on the outside wall by the arched front doorway out loud. Like the turret, the name seemed out of place.

Below the plaque, someone had scratched some words. Blythe looked closer. "Believe the legend."

Although the day had dawned bright and sunny, a chill suddenly came over her. She shivered, remembering a line from that long-ago teenager slasher movie she'd starred in with Drew Montgomery, about someone walking over her grave.

Shaking off the feeling, Blythe climbed the stairs to the third floor.

Cait answered at her first knock. Her bold grin revealed that she was reveling in her new assignment.

"I was hoping I'd arrive here and find out you'd changed your mind," Blythe said as they hugged.

"Not on a bet. This is a lifetime opportunity. I'd be a fool to pass it up."

"A live fool," Blythe pointed out. "To think your friends all worried when you were assigned to the decoy squad." Although Cait had insisted the Vice Squad duty was absolutely safe, Blythe had never quite believed that.

"Oh, this is lots better," Cait said.

She'd told Blythe about her new assignment to the fugitive squad last night on the phone, and although she hadn't gone into detail, what little she had said had left Blythe feeling horribly concerned.

From the bright gleam in Cait's green eyes, Blythe knew this latest assignment might be a great deal more dangerous than dressing up like Kathleen Turner in *Crimes of Passion* and sashaying up and down Hollywood Boulevard.

"I can't believe you're actually considering going undercover to catch a rapist."

"I'll fill you in on the details while I finish packing."

Blythe followed Cait into her bedroom and sat down on the edge of the lacy, white iron bed, watching as Cait took a hot pink sweater from a dresser drawer and added it to the jeans and underwear she'd already packed.

"Remember a few years ago, when that Surfer Rapist was running loose on the beach?"

"How could I forget?" The man had terrorized the beach communities for more than a year.

"Well, he escaped. And according to his cell mate, he's on his way back here."

"You'd think he'd want to get as far away from where he was arrested as possible."

Cait shrugged. "I guess, if he was a normal, clear think-ing kind of guy, he wouldn't be a serial rapist." An oversize gray LAPD T-shirt she liked to sleep in joined the sweater. "It gets worse."

"Terrific," Blythe muttered.

"Apparently, while he was locked up, he told more than one fellow prisoner that if he ever got out, he wasn't com-ing back. The trick, he decided, was not to leave any wit-nesses."

"Are you saying he intends to start killing his victims?"

"If you can believe these guys, and granted, they're not exactly boy scouts. But there isn't any real reason for them to lie. Everyone from the mayor to the police commissioner to the captains from every one of the beach cities all think he's deadly serious."

As Blythe considered that unsavory scenario, something flashed through her mind. "He was caught using a decoy, wasn't he?"

"A Venice detective from the squad's Rape and Domestic Violence Unit," Cait agreed. "Charity Prescott, who is cur-rently serving as police chief of Castle Mountain, Maine. Wherever the hell that is."

Blythe closed her eyes. When she opened them, she groaned as she viewed Cait's expression. She looked, Blythe considered, like a high-strung thoroughbred at the starting gate.

"That's why you're going to Maine, isn't it?" She rubbed at her temple, where a headache was beginning to threaten. "To learn how to draw the rapist out. To trick him into at-tacking you instead of a civilian."

"That's it in a nutshell." She tossed a pair of gray leg-gings into the suitcase.

Blythe sat still for a long silent moment, taking Cait's news in. Deep down, she'd suspected something like this last night, when Cait had first mentioned her latest undercover sting operation. But never would she have guessed that the man Cait and the team were trying to apprehend could be so brutally deadly.

"I hate the idea of you putting yourself in danger this way."

"It's my job."

"I know." Blythe had accepted that idea, even though she'd never quite gotten used to it. "But why couldn't you choose something safer? Like handing out parking tickets? Or hauling in little old ladies for jaywalking on Rodeo Drive."

Rather than take offense, as she would have if anyone else had suggested such a thing, Cait laughed. "Now you sound like my mother. Lord, maybe it's contagious."

They laughed together, the tension soothed. "I really do like your new place," Blythe said, looking around the cozy room. She'd always thought it an intriguing contrast that Cait, who, before her prostitute duty, went to work in a stark, unattractive dark blue uniform designed for men, returned home at the end of her shift to lacy furnishings that were a romantic tribute to the Victorian Age.

The white eyelet bedcover was adorned with deep ruffles and accented with decorative pillows. The walls were sprigged with tiny blue rosebuds and white lace filtered the bright California sunlight, allowing the dark green ivy plant hanging in front of the window to flourish. Roses bloomed on the blue needlepoint rug that covered most of the oak plank floor.

Against the sea of soft blues, a white wicker dressing table and chair created a peaceful oasis. An antique crocheted shawl had been draped over the bedside table and a white Victorian birdcage adorned the top of the ornate, Victorian bureau.

"I like it," Cait agreed, looking around with satisfaction. "Although it doesn't have the amenities of some of those huge complexes that are springing up like weeds—the ones with on-site gyms, party pavilions and volleyball courts— I fell in love with it at first sight."

She grinned at the memory of how she'd been driving down the street in her patrol car and had nearly caused a three-car pileup when she'd slammed on her brakes at the sight of the For Rent sign outside the gracefully aging pink building.

"I know it sounds like some of that La La Land New Age stuff, but the minute I saw it, I almost felt as if destiny had brought me here."

She laughed, sounding a little uncomfortable. "If I weren't such a feet-on-the-ground kind of woman, I'd almost believe the Bachelor Arms legend."

Her statement brought back to Blythe the words scratched below the apartment's name. *Believe the legend.* "What legend?"

"You're going to think I'm crazy."

"I already think you're crazy." This dangerous plan to capture the Surfer Rapist was proof of that.

"Well, according to legend, weird things have happened here, including some mysterious deaths. There's a mirror down in 1-G. I haven't seen it yet, but I've heard about it. Supposedly it's this huge pewter thing with lots of scrolls and rosebuds and stuff."

"Sounds like just your style."

"Doesn't it?" Cait shot a quick, appreciative glance at the gilded, ornately framed full-length mirror in the corner of the room. "Anyway, people say that sometimes you can see a woman in it." She grinned sheepishly. "I told you it was crazy."

"It sounds a little far-fetched," Blythe admitted. She picked up an old-fashioned snow globe from the bedside table, shook it gently and watched the white flakes drift down over the quaint little Victorian village inside. "But this certainly wouldn't be the first supposedly haunted house in town."

Three such cases that came immediately to mind were the house on Hollywood Boulevard where Ricky and David had grown up that was supposedly haunted with the ghost of Ozzie Nelson, George "Superman" Reeves's former home on Benedict Canyon and, of course, the burned ruins of Harry Houdini's estate.

"It gets even stranger," Cait revealed, on a light laugh designed to show that she didn't really believe in such supernatural goings-on. "There's also a legend that says if you see the woman in the mirror, your greatest wish could be granted. Or your greatest fear realized."

The words, casually spoken, struck some deep inner chord. Blythe was glad she was sitting down. The glass ball slipped through her suddenly frozen fingers. Fortunately it landed safely on the mattress and not on the wood floor.

"Blythe?" Cait was staring at her. "Are you all right?"

"I'm fine." When her voice broke, Blythe gave herself a minute to get her equilibrium back. "Really."

"You're as white as Ozzie Nelson's ghost."

Blythe refused to squirm beneath the worried, intense gaze. The hard, deep way Cait was looking at her reminded Blythe that this was a woman accustomed to getting the truth from people determined to lie.

"That's what I get for skipping lunch. Next time I'll at least get a candy bar at the commissary."

Personally, Cait thought that there was a lot more wrong with Blythe than a sudden sugar drop, but she'd known her friend long enough to know when not to pry. Something had happened. Something that had caused a faint, but unmistakable fear to haunt her dark eyes.

No, Cait corrected, not fear. Terror. Cait wondered if Blythe's reaction had to do with the news about the rapist. Or something else. Whatever it was, Blythe would tell her when she was ready.

Blythe watched Cait assess her words and was relieved when she decided not to push. An oddly strained silence settled over them.

A silence that was blessedly broken by the sudden burst of music filtering up from the apartment below. "Does this happen often?" Blythe asked.

"Every morning and every afternoon, like clockwork. In the beginning I was tempted to run the guy in for disturbing the peace, but—call me crazy—I've kind of gotten to like it." She grinned. "Let me tell you, it makes one helluva wake-up call."

"I can imagine." Blythe shook her head in a blend of amazement and admiration. They were having to shout to be heard over the blare. "I didn't even know it was possible to play 'Blue Suede Shoes' on a bagpipe."

"Wait until you hear 'Jailhouse Rock'," Cait advised.

On cue, the bagpipes moved on to the old Elvis hit.

"Amazing," Blythe shouted. "I think I've figured out the secret of Bachelor Arms."

"What's that?"

Blythe's grin chased away the lingering shadows in her eyes. "Elvis's ghost is living in apartment 2-C."

They laughed, the uncomfortable moment put away. For now.

As Cait finished packing, she filled Blythe in on the few tenants she'd met thus far.

"Jill's gorgeous. And a dead ringer for Linda Evans." She described the interior decorator who'd helped her arrange her furniture in her new apartment. "In fact, Saturday she was shopping at Vons and one of those celebrity look-alike agents came up to her and offered her a job, right there in the frozen food section."

"Did she accept?"

"Of course not." Cait grinned, knowing how Blythe reluctantly tolerated the two women who made their living cutting grand opening ribbons and appearing at parties posing as Blythe Fielding. "She told me she moved here from Boston after her divorce to reinvent herself. Not pretend to be someone else.

"Let's see. There's also Bobbie Sue and Brenda. They want to be actresses."

"Surprise, surprise."

"Don't be catty," Cait advised. "Not everyone is lucky enough to get the Ivory soap gig while still in the cradle. Anyway, I've only run into them in passing in the laundry room, but Jill says they're nice.

"Then there's this one old lady you've got to meet," Cait said. "Natasha Kuryan. She showed up my first night to welcome me with these sweet little almond cakes and tea in glasses."

"Like the Russians drink it," Blythe murmured, thinking of Alexandra Romanov.

"Exactly. Anyway, the woman's a treasure trove of gossip about the old days. Believe me, the sixties generation definitely did not invent the sexual revolution. According to Natasha, she had affairs with some of the town's biggest stars."

The name didn't ring a bell. Blythe wondered idly if the woman might have known Alexandra. "Did she marry any of them?"

"I don't think so. If she did, she hasn't mentioned it. It's my impression that Natasha was much too busy having fun to settle down with any one man. Not all women," she said pointedly, "view marriage as Valhalla."

"Not all women are so jaded," Blythe returned calmly, without heat. She was not about to get into another argument about Alan.

Cait opened her mouth to comment, then decided that Blythe knew her feelings regarding marriage in general and marriage to Alan Sturgess in particular.

In an unspoken agreement to change the subject, they continued to chat while Cait finished packing. The stream of consciousness conversation moved smoothly from world and national current affairs, to Blythe's successful, yet strangely unsettling meeting with Gage Remington, to what the weather might be in Castle Mountain, Maine, which they both guessed would be iffy this time of year, to Lily Van Cortlandt's arrival in Los Angeles.

Lily had still been Lily Padgett when the three young women became inseparable during their college days at Brown University. After graduating at the top of her class, she'd gone on to Harvard Law, where she'd fallen in love with J. Carter Van Cortlandt, the dashing scion of an old Manhattan banking and law family. Recently widowed, and pregnant with her first child, Lily was to be Blythe's bridesmaid.

"How did she sound when you talked with her the other night?" Cait called out from the bathroom where she was packing her toiletries.

"It's hard to tell. She said she and the baby are fine. But I thought I could hear an awful lot of stress in her voice."

"That's not surprising." Cait returned to the bedroom and zipped up the plain black soft-sided suitcase. "You're the actress, try putting yourself in her shoes.

"Your husband has been killed in a flaming car wreck that also took the life of his administrative assistant, with whom it turns out he was having a very public and very torrid affair while you played the lonely lady of the manor in Connecticut. Your inlaws still think of you as that usurping, corn-fed farm girl from Iowa who stole their precious baby boy out from under their aristocratic noses, and you're seven months pregnant.

"Don't you think you might be a little stressed out?"

"Of course." Blythe shook her head, thinking back on that unsatisfactory conversation with Lily. "But I still got the impression that something else is bothering her."

"As if that all weren't enough." Cait shrugged. "Well, whatever it is, I guess after she arrives in town, I'll just have to take her down to the station and bring out the bright lights and rubber hoses. That'll probably drag the truth out of her."

Blythe laughed. And continued to worry. About both her friends.

Cait finished packing in time for them to continue their conversation over glasses of white wine in the sunny living room.

"It's really nice of you to take me to the airport," Cait said again.

"It's no problem. I can drop you by LAX and still make my dinner with Walter Stern at L'Orangerie."

"Ah, the high octane of Hollywood deal making," Cait said, remembering the argument she'd witnessed between Blythe and the studio head yesterday at her mother's Brunch.

She wondered if things had been settled between them, considered asking, then reminded herself that she'd always tried to avoid anything to do with the business.

Besides, if it was important, Blythe would tell her. They'd always shared everything. "Makes me light-headed just to think of it."

"Somebody's got to make the movies," Blythe pointed out. "Or you wouldn't have been able to make out with Jimmy Jones in the back row of all those Westwood theaters."

"Got a point there," Cait agreed with another of those quick grins that lit up her face so that it seemed to glow from within.

Caitlin Carrigan had inherited the genes of one of the most gorgeous actresses ever to appear on the silver screen. But Blythe had always thought it was Cait's energetic, outgoing personality that made her truly beautiful.

As they left the building, they passed an open doorway on the first floor. As if her feet had been suddenly nailed to the spot, Blythe froze in front of the door.

Realizing Blythe was no longer beside her, Cait turned. "Blythe?" All the color had drained from her friend's face. "Are you all right?"

Embarrassed, Blythe gave herself a stiff mental shake. "Of course." But she still couldn't quite make herself move.

"Oh, this is the apartment I told you about," Cait said when she finally noticed the open door. "The one that's supposed to be haunted."

"The one with the mirror?"

"Exactly." Cait grinned. "I've been dying to see inside the place."

When she walked right in, Blythe hesitated, then followed.

The carpet was slightly damp, as if it had been recently shampooed. The mirror in question was impossible to miss. At least four feet wide and five feet high, it was every bit as elaborate as Cait had heard.

"Oh, I absolutely adore it," Cait said on a lustful sigh. "And it would look terrific in my bedroom. I wonder if it's for sale?"

"Not likely," a male voice suddenly spoke behind her.

Cait and Blythe both spun around, coming face-to-face with a short bald man. Cait's heart, which had trebled its beat, slowed when she recognized Ken Amberson, the building's super.

"Gracious, Ken," she said, "you surprised me." It was not the first time Cait had noticed the man's seeming ability to appear from nowhere. "I was cleaning the carpet." His gaze shifted to Blythe. "You're Blythe Fielding."

Accustomed to being recognized in public, Blythe flashed her vague, public smile. "Yes. I am."

"Ken Amberson," he introduced himself. "The super here. Saw your last film. Your performance was the only good thing about it."

"Thank you. I guess," Blythe murmured. Everyone, she'd discovered during a lifetime of acting, was a critic.

During the brief discourse, Cait wandered over to the wall and ran her fingers over the pewter scrolling. "Are you sure the owner of the building isn't interested in selling?"

"Wouldn't matter." Amberson shrugged. "Damn thing won't come off the wall," he elaborated at Cait's questioning look.

"That's impossible." Cait took hold of the frame and tugged. The mirror held fast to the wall. "Surely there's some way."

"Lots of folks have tried," he assured her. "None have succeeded."

"Well, they obviously didn't try the right thing," Cait argued. The longer she looked at the mirror, the more she wanted it for her own. "At the very least, you could tear down the wall."

"Maybe," he agreed with another shrug. "But it kind of belongs here." He turned to Blythe, giving her a long, probing look that made her want to squirm. "Wouldn't you say?"

The funny thing was, as spooky as the superintendent made her feel, Blythe found herself agreeing with him. There was something very right about the mirror's location. "It certainly is a focal point for the room."

"Well, I'm still going to check into it," Cait decided. "There's no harm in asking."

After saying goodbye to the superintendent, Blythe walked away, feeling strangely as if she were escaping something dark and dangerous.

This time it was Cait who paused in the open doorway, glancing back one last time at the mirror.

It was then she saw it.

Although she told herself that she had to be hallucinating, she couldn't drag her gaze away from the image of a woman, dressed in a long pale gown.

Their eyes met. The woman was looking at her as if she could see all the way to her soul. Then she smiled, a strange, sweet smile.

"Blythe."

Curious at the sudden stress in Cait's tone, Blythe turned around. "What is it?"

Before Cait could respond, the figure faded away, like a dream.

Cait shook her head. "Nothing. Never mind," she insisted at Blythe's quick, questioning look.

Telling herself that the reflected image had been nothing more than a product of her overly active imagination, stimulated by Ken Amberson's spooky presence, Cait shook her head once again to clear it, and followed Blythe out to the Jaguar parked at the curb.

They'd just left, en route to the airport, when the white limo carrying Natasha back from tea at the Regency glided into the vacated space at the curb.

7

THE DEPARTURE GATE for the American Airlines flight to Boston, from where she planned to connect with a commuter flight to Bangor, Maine, was crowded with people when Cait arrived. As she stood in line, she remained deep in thought about this latest assignment.

Blythe was right about it being dangerous, she admitted as the line inched its way forward to the check-in counter. But to earn a promotion to the Sex Crimes Unit, she'd be willing to parade naked in front of the devil himself.

Well, perhaps she wouldn't exactly go that far.

But as she handed her ticket to the young man behind the counter, responding absently to his cheery greeting and assuring him that a window seat would be fine, she considered that there wasn't much she wouldn't do to win the long-coveted slot. Cait sat in a molded plastic chair by the window to await boarding. Nearby a young boy was running back and forth in front of the glass wall, arms outstretched, pretending to be one of the jets that was taking off and landing just outside. Cait barely noticed. She was thinking about what little she'd been told about Charity Prescott.

She certainly didn't know much, although a phone call to Gage, who'd worked briefly in Venice before moving to LAPD, and a few more to acquaintances in the seaside town's police department had filled her in on some sketchy details.

Before becoming a cop, Charity had worked as a lawyer for Legal Aid, one source had told her. But apparently the system moved too slowly for the idealistic attorney, so she'd decided she could help people more by becoming a cop and putting the bad guys behind bars.

She quickly worked her way up from patrol to detective without, it seemed, making a single enemy. Everyone Cait had spoken with had described the woman as dedicated, hardworking, courageous and caring, while at the same time pragmatic enough to do the job without burning out.

It had been her idea to go undercover, posing as a beach bunny—the rapist's usual target—to draw him out of hiding. And it had worked.

She'd gone on to work as an advisor for a television series, surprising everyone when she'd married Steven Stone, the weekly program's star. No one who knew Stone's well-deserved reputation as a womanizer was surprised when six months later, Charity divorced the actor.

Surprising everyone again, she'd moved to Castle Mountain, a small town located on a remote island off the coast of Maine. An office pool had been established in the Venice PD as to how soon she'd be back. Most of her fellow officers figured she'd last out in those icy boondocks a month. Two years later, she was still there. Gage had told Cait he'd heard Charity had married again.

Cait, who thrived on the excitement that was part and parcel of working on a big city police force could not imagine moving to the boondocks where police calls undoubtedly consisted of barking dog complaints and Saturday night teenage vandalism.

As she rose in response to the boarding call and handed her pass to the uniformed clerk at the gate, she wondered exactly what she was going to find when she arrived in Castle Mountain.

Was Charity Prescott a typical burnout case? The thought worried her as she walked briskly down the jetway. Was she going to turn out to be one of those cops who just sat around the office all day, drinking coffee and swapping stories about the old days while her sidearm rusted away in a desk drawer?

Had she ceased to care?

No, Cait decided. During their brief telephone conversation this afternoon, Charity Prescott Valderian—it turned out that she *had* remarried—had sounded honestly interested in helping capture the man she'd risked her life to apprehend. She'd also sounded furious that he'd been allowed to escape.

Cait boarded the plane. Checking her seat assignment for the first time, she saw that she was in seat 4-A. When she glanced around and located her seat, her first thought was that the man at the counter had made a mistake. When she saw who was to be sitting next to her, her second thought was that she was going to kill Sloan Wyndham.

His smile was slow and lacking a single ounce of contrition.

This was so damn typical, Cait thought angrily. It was exactly the kind of exaggerated gesture one of her parents would have made. The same brash, larger-than-life Hollywood grandstanding she'd spent her entire life trying to get away from.

Furious, she spun around and thrust her boarding pass at the flight attendant who was welcoming people aboard. "There's been a mistake."

One perfectly plucked brow arched. "Oh, dear." Full red lips that matched her scarf turned down in a moue. "Is someone in your seat?"

"That's the problem," Cait said. "It's not my seat."

"Are you certain?"

"Positive."

Sighing at Cait's no-nonsense tone, the flight attendant tapped away at a small onboard computer. "I'm sorry, Ms. Carrigan," she said. "But 4-A is correct."

The woman glanced down the aisle at the wide leather seat that remained unoccupied. And would for the entire flight, if Cait had anything to say about it. "Would you prefer an aisle? Perhaps the gentleman in 4-B would be willing to change—"

"What I would prefer is my proper seat."

"But 4-A is your proper seat."

"Fine." Cait forced a smile. "Then I'd like to change. To Coach."

"I'm sorry. But this is a full flight. There aren't any open seats in coach."

"What about my old one?"

More tapping. "It's been filled by a standby passenger."

Cait's eyes whipped back to Sloan. The man had the cockiest, most infuriating grin. "Surely someone will be willing to change. If you ask."

"I'm sorry." The attendant shook her head, causing her short blond curls to bounce energetically. "But we're already two minutes late taking off and the captain is getting impatient."

She glanced behind her at the half open door of the cockpit. Inside, Cait could see the crew running through their preflight check. "If you could please just take your seat, perhaps after we're in the air—"

"Never mind." The entire scenario was becoming more trouble than it was worth. If she continued to complain, Sloan might get the outlandish idea that she was actually intimidated by the idea of sitting beside him on the long cross-country flight.

Cait stomped back to the seat. Before she could put her carry-on bag in the overhead compartment, Sloan was on his feet, taking it from her hand and lifting it up with ease.

"That wasn't necessary."

"It was if we want to take off," he responded easily. "Or would you rather keep it beneath the seat in front of you?"

"I'd rather put it away in coach." Her foot began to tap. "Where it—and I—belong."

She was furious. Heat waves were radiating from her and her remarkable eyes were shooting emerald sparks. Sloan couldn't recall ever meeting a more passionate woman.

"Lord, you fire up quick." He wondered idly if she'd prove as hot in bed and figured she would. The trick would be not setting the sheets on fire.

"Only when provoked."

Seeing the attendant headed her way and realizing she was about to be reminded of the captain's impatience, Cait pushed past him, settled into the wide tan seat with a furious flounce and fastened her seat belt.

"Guess I should be grateful they don't let you carry your police pistol on board." Unperturbed, Sloan sat back down beside her. "Excuse me, but—"

"Not in a million years." She was looking out the window, pretending vast interest in the ground crew loading luggage onto a DC-10 at the adjoining gate.

"What?"

His hand was on her leg. Her head spun back toward him as she knocked it aside. "I will not excuse you for manipulating me like this for a million—a billion—years."

"As discouraging a threat as that is, I was merely trying to point out that you're sitting on half of my seat belt."

"Oh." Refusing to reveal her embarrassment, she cleared her throat and lifted her hips. "I'm sorry."

"No problem." He tugged it free and fastened it with a decisive snap. The motion drew her gaze to his hands. For a brief, weakening moment Cait found herself wondering exactly how those dark hands would feel against her naked skin, searching out forbidden secrets.

No! This had to stop. She couldn't allow herself to continually fantasize about this man who was so horribly wrong for her.

She had a job to do. People were depending on her. So many people she couldn't begin to count them all. But mostly, she had to keep a clear head so that some innocent woman would not end up being raped. And killed.

Sloan watched the emotions flood into her eyes. Reluctant desire, irritation, resolve. When he'd called Blythe last night, making up some cockamamy excuse about double-checking the time of their lunch meeting—which had made him feel ridiculously as if he were in high school—in order to slip in a seemingly innocuous question about Cait, she'd told him about the trip to Maine.

He'd immediately called the airport, deciding fate was working in his favor when he'd discovered there were two seats available in first class. He immediately booked one for himself and changed Cait's economy class seat to the second.

Truthfully, he hadn't exactly expected her to welcome him with open arms. But after those shared kisses, he wasn't prepared for her to treat him like Jack the Ripper, either.

She'd turned away again. Although she'd pulled her hair into a twist at the top of her head, a few errant strands had escaped to trail down the back of her neck.

Unable to resist, he twined one of those long fiery strands of hair around a finger.

He felt her tense and dropped his hand before she could light into him. She shot him a look. "Are you trying to annoy me, Mr. Wyndham?"

"As a matter of fact, it seems I don't have to try." Sloan liked the contrast between those cool round tones and the heat in her eyes. A man who admittedly bored easily, his interest could only be held by a complex woman. "It seems to come naturally." His grin was slow and knowing and infuriated Cait anew. "Gum?"

"No, thank you." She refused the red pack with the haughty disregard of a duchess. Sloan almost applauded the performance then decided not to push his luck.

"Are you sure? Sometimes it helps—"

"I said I don't want any damn gum." The duchess was gone and in her place was a short-tempered female who could test the mettle of any man.

Sloan grinned again, reminding himself that he'd always enjoyed a challenge. "Suit yourself." He unwrapped a piece, popped it into his mouth and began to chew, the cocky, masculine grin never fading from his face.

When she felt her own lips starting to tug in a reluctant, answering smile, Cait turned away again, watching the terminal grow smaller as the jet taxied down the runway.

Neither spoke during takeoff. Nor for several minutes afterward. Once they were airborne, the flight attendant served drinks—white wine for Cait, Scotch for Sloan. When the blonde's dazzling, Miss America smile seemed to flash a little brighter at Sloan, Cait experienced a disturbing little pang of jealousy, the same as she'd felt at the sight of her mother's slender hand resting on his arm.

"Cheers." He turned toward her, lifting the heavy glass.

Cait refused to acknowledge the toast. "What do you think you're doing on this flight?"

He lowered the glass without comment and took a sip. "I don't suppose you'd believe I had a sudden yen for a vacation."

She shook her head. "Not a chance."

"Perhaps I'm researching a story."

She thought about that, eyeing him over the rim of her wineglass. "Better. But I still find it difficult to buy. Especially when you're supposed to be working on Blythe's screenplay."

The answer to the question she'd been asking herself hit her. "That's how you found out about this trip, isn't it? From Blythe."

"Don't blame her," he said. "She just happened to mention it in passing. The rest—" he waved his hand, his slight gesture encompassing the plane, their seats, and this unscheduled, impulsive trip—was all my idea."

"A stupid idea," she muttered.

"Actually, I thought it was one of my more brilliant ones."

"Well, it's not."

"We needed to talk," Sloan said. "I had the feeling you'd just keep walking out on me, which is a bit difficult to do at 30,000 feet."

"Now there's where you've miscalculated. I may not be able to walk out, but there's no way you can make me listen to anything you have to say."

To prove her point, she took the headphones from the seatback in front of her, slammed them onto her head and tuned to the soft favorites channel in the hopes the easy listening music would cool her irritation.

Knowing that it was a long flight, Sloan reminded himself that patience was reputed to be a virtue. He shrugged, took out his laptop computer and began to write the opening scene of his screenplay.

Since he'd culled the story of Alexandra and Patrick's argument at the Hearst beach house the night of the murder from microfilm in the *L.A. Times* morgue, he'd decided to begin his movie with that and work his way back in time.

Beside him, Cait sat with her head against the back of the seat, eyes closed, ignoring him as if he were invisible.

Dinner—a shellfish tamale, salad and blue corn chips with guacamole—had been served and eaten, trays had been taken away and coffee poured before Cait finally surrendered.

They'd just passed over the Mississippi River when she took off those earphones Sloan was beginning to hate and turned toward him.

"What else did Blythe say?"

"About Alexandra Romanov?"

"No. About me."

"Ah."

He leaned back in his seat, crossed his legs at the ankles and sipped his coffee thoughtfully. He thought about asking why, if she honestly didn't care anything about him, she cared what he knew about her, then decided that he wasn't up to playing any more games where the delectable Cait Carrigan was concerned.

"Now that you mention it, I seem to recall something about you being about to risk that lovely neck again."

Cait's temper flared predictably. "She had no right to tell you about that!"

Sloan shrugged. "She's worried about you. And for that matter, so am I."

"Why?"

"She's your best friend—"

"Not Blythe. I know why she's concerned. I was referring to you."

"Oh. Beats me." He rubbed at the gathering tension at the back of his neck. "I suppose, the appropriate thing for me to say is that as a fellow human being, I'd worry about anyone who was about to set herself up as a target for some psychopathic rapist."

Cait nodded. "I suppose that makes sense."

"Perfect sense," Sloan agreed. He stared past her, out the oval window at the sky that had turned inky black. Inside the cabin the flight crew had dimmed the lights. "The problem is that it's not the truth. Not the whole truth, anyway."

He tossed off the rest of the cooling coffee and returned the cup to the flight attendant passing by before answering.

"The truth is—" he turned back to her, his whiskey brown eyes holding her reluctant gaze hostage "—you triggered something in me, Cait. From the moment I looked down from the top of Blythe's gate and saw you standing there, dressed like any red-blooded male's most erotic fantasy, which, let me tell you, made one helluva contrast with that deadly 9mm pistol you were pointing in my direction."

"I thought you were a burglar."

"Makes sense to me." He leaned closer and treated her to another one of those slow, sensual grins that once again made her pulse leap.

He leaned closer still. Sloan watched the awareness flood into her eyes, understood that she would have run away if only there'd been anywhere to run.

Congratulating himself on arranging this stolen time together, he bent his head and touched his mouth to hers.

When he felt her shudder, he cupped her cheek in his palm.

"You are so sweet," he murmured against her lips. Although he'd never believed in heaven, Sloan now knew what it tasted like. "You quite literally take my breath away."

She also made him feel sixteen again. Sixteen and horny, but he decided, for the sake of discretion, not to mention that salient little fact.

"Don't talk to me that way," she protested even as she melded into the light kiss. Her soft voice, almost a whisper, could barely be heard over the drone of the jet engines. "I don't want this."

"I know." He could feel the ache deep within every bone of his body. His mouth whispered over hers. "But sometimes what we want—" his fingers trailed up her cheek as his lips continued to pluck seductively at hers "—and what we get are two entirely different things."

He was doing it again! Cait's head was spinning, her bones were melting, and her heart was pounding like a jackhammer. This simply had to stop, she told herself weakly. She couldn't keep putting herself at risk like this.

Because every feminine instinct she possessed told her that in his own way, this man was every bit as hazardous as the Surfer Rapist she'd vowed to apprehend.

Sloan Wyndham was dangerous.

And heaven help her, against all reason, she wanted him.

Reckless, she ignored the voice of caution trying to make itself heard in the far reaches of her mist-hazed mind and dragged her hands through his dark hair. Desperate, she forgot all the reasons why this was a fatal mistake and allowed herself to sink deeper and deeper into Sloan's seductive kiss.

When Cait's ripe, succulent lips parted on a soft moan, encouraging him to deepen the kiss, Sloan ripped away the little twist of lace that held her hair in that topknot, allowing it to pour over her shoulders, where the spicy scent of it infiltrated its way into his senses like an inhaled drug.

When he finally surrendered her lips, her eyes remained glazed with a reluctant desire she could no longer deny. In his, a flame continued to burn brightly.

"I don't understand." She dragged a trembling hand through her tangled hair, then dropped it weakly. Her voice was weak and tattered. She was trembling.

Because he could not remain this close to Cait without touching her, Sloan ran both his wide hands across her shoulders, than down her arms, the gesture meant to soothe, rather than arouse. "Believe me, Cait, you're not alone there."

His heart was still beating too fast and too hard. What was it about Cait Carrigan that could tie him into such tight, painful knots?

"I think, when we land in Boston, you should book the next flight home." Even as Cait said the words, Sloan felt something from her, a lingering desire that told him it was not her first choice.

"Sorry. But I've always wanted to see Maine."

She stiffened at his cocky, I-do-whatever-I-want tone. Reminding herself of the reason for this trip cleared the cobwebs from her mind. "Look, I have work to do in Maine. I can't allow you to interfere."

"No problem. I have no intention of interfering in your work."

"You already have," she snapped. Deciding since she'd already gone this far, she may as well admit to the havoc he was causing to her senses, she said, "I can't think straight if you keep kissing me like that."

"Fine." Although his body still ached with unsatiated need, Sloan smiled. He hadn't expected her to admit to so much so soon. "How about I promise to refrain from kissing you during working hours?"

"No good." She shook her head, knowing that she'd spend all her time either remembering earlier kisses or anticipating those not yet shared. "You have to stop kissing me. Or at least until after I've had my meeting with Charity Prescott."

She may as well ask the sun to stop rising in the morning. Or the sea to stop its eternal ebb and flow.

"It's either that, or I'll have to you run in for obstructing justice."

Figuring he'd love to see her explain that charge to some rural Maine constable, Sloan decided not to argue. Blythe had already stressed how seriously Cait took her work, something he'd witnessed firsthand during that brief exchange with her mother. If he forced her to choose, Sloan wasn't certain—at least at this point in their relationship—that he'd end up the winner.

"You drive a hard bargain, Officer."

She folded her arms across her chest and felt her equilibrium beginning to return. "Take it or leave it."

Although it was not his first choice, Sloan reminded himself that once she'd had her meeting with Castle Mountain's lady police chief, all bets were off.

"Lady," he said, "you've got yourself a deal."

Cait desperately wanted to believe him. Desperately needed to believe him.

As the plane began its descent into Boston's Logan Airport, she forced her mind back onto her all-important mission and tried, with scant success, to ignore the faint twinges of foreboding caused by the masculine gleam in Sloan's whiskey-hued eyes.

8

IT WAS NOT AN EASY TRIP. After landing in Boston, Sloan and Cait boarded a commuter jet to Bangor. In Bangor, they found the charter pilot Charity had promised would be waiting to take them to Castle Mountain. There was a ferry, she'd explained to Cait on the phone, however it only ran weekly until the summer tourist season.

It was past midnight when they touched down on the small landing strip and found a driver from the Gaslight Inn waiting. Cait was grateful when the man turned out to be a stereotypical taciturn New Englander. She was so exhausted, she was no longer able to think, let alone manage any type of coherent conversation.

The owner of the inn was waiting up as well, although the flannel robe the woman was wearing suggested she'd been awakened by the call from the pilot informing her of Cait and Sloan's pending arrival. The old-fashioned parlor, which functioned as a lobby, was filled to the brim with Victorian and European furnishings Cait knew she would find delightful, if she weren't so sleepy.

Sloan was as dead on his feet as Cait. But after having had her head on his shoulders during the flight from Bangor—she'd drifted off immediately after takeoff—and having inhaled her spicy scent at such close range, he was uncomfortably wired.

He declined the obviously sleepy owner's offer to show them to their rooms, assuring her that they were more than capable of managing on their own.

For once Cait didn't fight him when he scooped up both their bags. Desperately fighting to keep her eyes open, she dragged herself up the stairs.

The rooms were next door to one another. Sloan stopped at the first door and unlocked it. "Good night."

"'Night." She took her carry-on bag and turned to go in, but at the last minute he stopped her.

"Wait a minute. I forgot something."

Cait glanced back over her shoulder. "What?"

Okay, so he was going to break the rules. But what the hell. He couldn't help himself. Soft and flushed with sleep, Cait was the most delectable sight he'd ever seen.

"This." His hand cupped her nape, sliding into her unbound hair. He bent his head. The touch of his lips on hers was as soft as dandelion fuzz, as brief as a heartbeat. Cait knew she was in deep, deep trouble when the light kiss caused her blood to thrum.

She was looking up at him with confusion and, dammit, Sloan thought, that painfully seductive, reluctant desire shining in her emerald eyes. It would be so easy, he mused. A few more lingering kisses, a tender touch here—his gaze skimmed over her breasts—another there—her hips—some seductive words, and she'd fall into his hands like a succulent, ripe plum.

But then what?

As impossible as it seemed, Sloan Wyndham, a man infamous for his hot, short, hit-and-run relationships, suddenly found himself wanting more. Much, much more.

He smiled. At her, at himself, at this ridiculous situation. "Good night."

She was pressing her fingers against her still parted lips, as if trying to hold in the heat. "'Night." She turned and disappeared into the room.

When she closed the door behind her, Sloan heard the click of the lock and realized that he hadn't known it was possible to feel both regret and relief at the same time.

After a frustrating night spent tossing and turning, staring up at the ceiling, imagining Cait warm and oh, so inviting in his bed, Sloan rose early and took a solitary walk along the rock-strewn beach.

The day had dawned cold and foggy, preventing him from seeing more than a few feet in front of him. But that didn't stop Sloan from sensing her approach. It was as if he possessed some type of internal radar that alerted him whenever Cait Carrigan came into kissing range.

"We need to talk." She was wearing a hooded, crimson jacket every bit as assertive as her tone.

"Good morning to you, too."

"We had a deal," she ground out, refusing to acknowledge his easy greeting. Her hands were jammed deep into her pockets, but from the fire in her eyes and the steel in her tone he suspected if she pulled them out, they'd be curled into fists. "You broke the rules last night."

"What rules were those?"

She threw her chin up in a way that told him unequivocally that she wasn't buying his innocent act for a second. "I distinctly recall you promising not to kiss me until I finished my business with the police chief."

"Perhaps you were dreaming."

"Not likely."

"I don't suppose you'd believe that I thought *I* was dreaming."

"No. I wouldn't."

"I didn't think so, but it was worth a try." He shrugged, then extended his arms, wrists together. "I give up. You may as well throw the cuffs on me again and drag me in, Officer.

Because it seems I have no choice but to plead guilty and throw myself on the mercy of the court."

Didn't he take anything seriously?

"This case is important to me, dammit!" Her shout scattered some gulls that had been wading in the surf at the edge of the rocky shore, searching out clams. "It's my ticket to what I've been working toward for years. I don't have the time or the inclination to get involved in a relationship!"

The long lonely night spent fantasizing about making love to Cait took its toll. Sloan's own temper sparked as well. "Tough. Because don't look now, lady, but you're already involved. All the way up to that fragrant neck."

Unfortunately, the words were all too true. Her irritation deflated, like air seeping out of a balloon. Cait shook her head and looked away.

"I really don't want this."

Another shrug. "Neither did I, in the beginning."

She gave him a sharp look, studied his open expression and decided he was telling the truth. "You make it sound as if we're nothing more than puppets with Fate pulling the strings."

Aptly put, Sloan decided, thinking over this past week.

"People have choices, Sloan," Cait said when he didn't answer.

She saw it every day in her work. Human beings had been created with a free will that made them choose to be either one of the good guys or one of the bad guys. These days, unfortunately, more and more people seemed to be taking the low road.

"Events don't happen in a vacuum," she insisted. "We have ultimate control over our lives."

"I used to think that." He met her earnest gaze with an unwavering one of his own. "I'm not sure I do anymore."

"That's ridiculous. I've always known what I wanted."

He didn't doubt her for a minute. But he did think if Cait actually believed she could turn her back on whatever it was that was happening between them, she was fooling herself.

"And if wants change?" he suggested quietly.

"Mine won't." Even as she said it, Cait knew it was a lie. Because heaven help her, she was starting to want Sloan. Too much for her own good.

"Want to know what I want?" he asked.

"No." She jammed her hands deeper into her pockets and turned away again, staring out at the bank of soft gray fog.

"Too bad. Because I'm going to tell you anyway."

He came up behind her, put his arms around her waist and drew her back against him. The sea air was damp and cold. She tried to concentrate on the chill even as the heat emanating from his body seeped seductively into her bones.

"I want to go back to the inn, carry you upstairs, light a fire in the stone fireplace, and spend a very long time undressing you. Piece by piece. Beginning with that red as sin coat and ending with whatever little scrap of silk and lace I suspect you're wearing beneath those jeans."

"Dammit, Sloan—"

"And then," he continued, as if he hadn't even heard her faint complaint, "I want to touch you, Cait. All over. And I want to taste you. Everywhere."

Heaven help her, that was precisely what she wanted him to do! It was the same thing he'd done last night in her unbelievably erotic dream that had left her hot and shaken and, dammit, wanting this morning.

"Sloan—" His name came out on a ragged protest.

He turned her in his arms, looked down into her upturned face and knew he was not alone in these unruly feelings. "And then I want you to touch me. Everywhere. And taste me, all over.

"And when we've both made each other crazy out of our minds, I want to bury myself deep inside your warm and welcoming body and I want us both to fly higher and longer than we've ever flown before and finally, when we come back to earth I want to do the same thing all over again. And again. And again.

"Until we're both too satisfied and too exhausted to move."

The sensual images his words painted weakened her knees. She closed her eyes and leaned her forehead against his shoulder. "This is impossible."

"No." He cupped her chin with the gentle touch she'd first been surprised to discover, and lifted her wary gaze to his. "Unexpected, perhaps. But not impossible."

They stood there, a breath apart, surrounded by the misty silver cloud of fog, alone on the rock-strewn expanse of beach save for the gulls and some sandpipers. They could have been the last two people on earth. The last woman. The last man.

In her eyes he saw a reflection of his own desperate needs, his own raw yearnings. And one last rebellious spark that flickered out even as he watched. Although she'd given it her best shot, Sloan knew that Cait could no longer deny what was happening between them. Not when faced with such elemental power.

The dark, sensual messages swirling between them were almost too much to bear. Her imagination fired by his sensual description of what he wanted to do to her, what he wanted them to do together, Cait's lips parted, her already slumberous eyes softened.

Forgetting his promise, choosing instead to respond to Cait's unspoken request, Sloan surrendered to temptation and kissed her.

The slow ache inside Sloan instantly turned painful. Desire suddenly had claws—sharp, fatal talons that were ripping at his heart, his gut. And lower.

It was happening to him all over again. Sloan had never been with a woman who could cause his hunger to spin so quickly and so dangerously out of control.

Never had he craved so deeply. Or so painfully. Cait Carrigan was the kind of woman who could make a man crawl on his knees over broken glass and relish the journey.

When her ripe, succulent lips parted on a soft moan, encouraging him to deepen the kiss, Sloan's mouth turned ravenous. He took everything she was offering, then demanded more. Their breathing was hot and ragged. Her taste, as rich and sweet and hot as it was, was not enough. As the building heat exploded inside him, Sloan covered her face with hot rough kisses. He wanted to thrust up that sweater she was wearing beneath her jacket and bury his mouth against the softness of her breasts.

When he found himself desperately needing to bury the aching, throbbing part of his anatomy into an equally soft and silky place, he knew that he was on the rocky edge of losing it completely.

Cait was on the brink of begging him to take her back to the inn to end this torment when the alarm on her watch suddenly sounded.

Realization came slowly. Reluctantly.

Sloan dragged his gaze from her ravaged lips back to her eyes. "Saved by the bell." His resigned tone was tinged with irony.

"What if I didn't want to be saved?" she asked with a flash of her characteristic spirit.

Her question told him what her eyes had already revealed. That if he'd asked her to return to the inn to make love with him, Cait would not have said no.

There had been a time when a few hours spent tangling the sheets with a woman like Cait would have satisfied him. When a brief, no-strings affair where both participants knew the score was more the norm than the exception. But that was before promiscuity could end up getting you killed.

Before AIDS.

And even more importantly, before Cait. Somehow, without him even being aware of it happening, Cait Carrigan had changed Sloan. She'd made him want more from a relationship than mutually enjoyable sex. She'd made him want more from a woman than an ego boost. And she'd made him want more from himself than a smooth line and a slow hand.

A brief affair with Cait, as pleasurable as he had no doubt it would be, would not even begin to be enough. What he wanted, Sloan realized, as the awareness hit him like a sharp axe between the eyes, was a lifetime.

"I've heard," he suggested with a wry twist of his firm lips, "that patience is perceived to be a virtue."

She'd been told the same thing innumerable times. "Do you believe that?" she asked with an arched brow.

He laughed, a deep, husky laugh that possessed the power to thrill. "Hell, no."

His head swooped down and he gave her another long, hot kiss that only left her wanting more. When they finally came up for air, he was smiling.

"But," he decided reluctantly, "I suppose there might be something to be said for anticipation." Although, other than an aching groin and teeth worn to the gums by gritting them hour after hour on end, Sloan wasn't exactly sure what.

"This is going to complicate things." At a time when her life was already too complicated as it was.

"Probably." He ran the back of his hand up the delicate curve of her cheek, pleased by the soft bloom of color caused by the light caress.

"I don't have time for distractions."

He managed, just barely, to dismiss his annoyance at having been referred to as a *distraction*. "How about this?" he suggested, pushing her hood back and catching her ear-lobe between his teeth. "Does this distract you?"

"Dammit, Sloan—"

"And this." His tongue trailed down the side of her neck. "Is this a distraction?"

They were standing so close together their knees touched. Although she was struggling to concentrate, Cait could feel the warmth emanating from his body, seeping into hers. "You know it is."

Her legs were trembling. She was trembling. Sinking even as she struggled to find solid ground. Because she was no longer certain she could stand on her own, Cait curled her hands around his shoulders.

"This isn't what I came here for."

He lifted his head and gave her a long, unfathomable look.

"No," Sloan said slowly, reminding himself that he'd never trusted things that came too easily. "It isn't. And so, to prove my good intentions, though I'm sorely tempted to drag you back to my lonely, unmade bed, I suppose I'd better let you leave for your meeting."

Cait was undeniably pleased at the way he was demonstrating respect for her work. His stroking fingers were creating little sparks on her skin, on her cheeks, her chin, her temple. "What will you do?"

"Do?" he asked distractedly.

Her creamy skin fascinated him. Although it looked like fragile, translucent porcelain, it was every bit as soft as silk.

Sloan was literally aching to explore the sensual phenomenon further.

When those wonderfully wicked fingers trailed with tantalizing slowness around the curve of her jawline, Cait sighed and tilted her head back to allow them access to her throat.

"While I'm at the police station." The fog surrounding them had filtered into her mind, wrapping her thoughts in misty clouds. It was difficult to think. It was nearly impossible to talk. Cait felt his thumb pause at the base of her throat and worried he could feel the increased beat of her blood.

Sloan could. The hot, hungry pulse echoed the out-of-control rhythm of his own. "I figured I'd spend the morning beneath a cold shower. Afterward, with luck, I may actually manage to get some writing done. And then, if you're still not back, I'll go swimming."

"Swimming?" She'd admittedly been exhausted last night, but she was sure she would have remembered the owner mentioning an indoor pool. She glanced past his shoulder at the churning white surf that would undoubtedly be as cold as a glacier this time of year. "Surely not—"

"In the sea," he agreed with a quick grin. "I figured, if that won't do the job, nothing will."

CHARITY PRESCOTT Valderian's office turned out to be every bit as warm and friendly as the woman herself. Instead of the usual police mug shots adorning the walls, she'd hung several paintings of the island.

A framed photo of a man clad in a police uniform hung behind her desk; although his hair was a darker auburn than the current police chief's, from his intelligent blue eyes and warm smile, Cait guessed she was looking at Charity's father.

Other photos lined the walls as well, but here again Charity proved her individuality. Cait had been told she'd received a medal from the Venice Police Chief as well as commendations from the mayors of Santa Monica, Venice, and L.A. for having apprehended the Surfer Rapist, but they were nowhere to be seen. Obviously, she'd chosen to forego the usual police chief's vanity wall.

Rather, the wall was a family gallery. Cait viewed a dated wedding photo of a lovely young woman and the man she'd guessed was Charity's father hanging beside another photo taken of the same woman several years later, marrying another man whose dark skin, rugged features, western-cut suit and dress black Stetson practically shouted out *rancher*.

There were more photos: Charity and some handsome man whom Cait guessed to be her current husband, Charity and that same man caught in a series of intimate poses chronicling the growth of their son from infancy to toddler.

There were photos of children—three look-alike little girls and a little boy, she guessed to be Charity with her sisters and brother. There was a wedding photo of that same brother and a lovely, serene-looking blonde and another of the couple proudly showing off a baby clad in a long, antique lace christening gown.

Along with the family photos were framed crayon drawings obviously done by a child. Charity's child, Cait suspected.

"Not exactly a typical police rogue's gallery," Charity allowed when she saw Cait examining the wall. "But then again, there's not much typical about Castle Mountain." Her grin was quick and friendly. "Besides, to tell you the truth, I've never quite understood why cops would want to spend their days looking at felons."

"This is certainly more uplifting," Cait agreed.

Another grin, even brighter than the first. "We're kind of big on family around here."

"I can see that." Studying the pictures, Cait felt a twinge of envy at the open emotion revealed in the subjects' faces. They looked so happy. So pleased with themselves. So pleased with one another. They all looked, she considered, so very much in love.

Cait had grown up understanding that relationships were, at best, transitory. That people came together because of mutual attraction and when that attraction faded, they moved on to greener pastures.

And although she didn't exactly condemn such practices—how could she, without condemning her parents, whom she loved, despite their foibles?—Cait had also decided long ago that such serial relationships were not for her.

Which, following that feeling to its logical conclusion, meant that she'd always viewed marriage with disdain.

But now, as she took in Charity's family wall and saw the glow of pride and love as the police chief showed off her husband and child, Cait experienced a faint flicker of doubt.

One thing she had no doubt about was Charity Prescott Valderian's dedication to law enforcement. Contrary to her earlier worries, the police chief was definitely not a burnout case. In fact, Cait couldn't remember when she'd met anyone who so enjoyed her work.

"Of course," Charity allowed, refilling Cait's coffee cup, "being a cop in Castle Mountain is a lot less stressful than being a cop in L.A."

She sat back down in the high-backed leather chair, took a sip of the strong coffee and grinned. "Fights over lobster traps, the occasional drunk and disorderly and domestic disputes are about as exciting as it gets around here."

That wasn't exactly what the pilot of the charter plane had said last night. "I heard something about you breaking a spy ring?"

To Cait's surprise, a shutter came down over Charity's intelligent blue eyes. She ran her hand through her short, sleek coppery hair and shrugged.

"It wasn't that big a deal. My brother Dylan, that's him with his wife, Julianna," she pointed to one of the more recent wedding photographs, "runs a think tank out in the woods. A rival scientist was trying to steal some secrets."

Another shrug. "It was more a case of industrial tampering than spying. You know how people exaggerate things in a small town," Charity explained easily.

Her tone was mild, her expression pleasant. Cait's cop's instincts, which were seldom wrong, told her there was more to the story than what she was hearing. Admittedly curious, she reminded herself that whatever had happened out at what her pilot, and apparently, the rest of the island referred to as The Brain Factory, was not what she'd come to Castle Mountain to learn.

"Actually, I don't know anything about small towns. Not firsthand, anyway," Cait said. "I was born in L.A." Deciding that it was time to get down to the reason for this trip, she leaned forward and said, "I'm planning to go undercover to catch him."

Charity nodded. "I thought that was your intention when you called and said you wanted to talk to me about him." She ran a finger thoughtfully around her cup. "Although it seems I could have told you everything I know over the phone."

"Not everything."

Cait had all the vital statistics from his yellow sheet. She knew the rapist's height, weight, MO. She knew his mother had abandoned him at birth, knew he'd been married three times, knew two of his former wives had testified that he'd abused them during their marriages.

The third wife, who'd been living in a shelter for battered women at the time, had been too terrified to come forward willingly. The woman assistant district attorney had decided that to issue a subpoena for her to appear was not only cruel, but unnecessary. They had enough to convict Henry McCrea without her. They had enough to put him away for life.

Unfortunately, he'd proven himself as slippery as he was evil and on a trip to court where he'd been expected to present a lawsuit against the prison cafeteria for denying him vegetarian meals, he'd escaped.

"I have the court testimony, including the psychologist's reports," Cait said. "But you're the one who really knows him. You're the one who knows how to push the bastard's buttons."

Charity steepled her fingers together and shifted her gaze to the photo of Prescott and Starbuck she'd taken during the brief ferry ride to the mainland just last weekend.

What a difference a few years made, she mused. At the time she'd willingly—eagerly—put her life in danger, apprehending the man who'd been terrorizing the beach cities up and down the coast.

She'd been frightened, she remembered. But pumped. Catching the bad guys had always given her a rush. But not nearly the rush she received when her child smiled at her. Or when her brilliant husband, home from his work at The Brain Factory, greeted her with a kiss that still possessed the power to curl her toes.

"Did they tell you he'd threatened to kill me?" she asked. "Yes."

Charity returned her gaze to Cait's, viewed the determination in those intelligent green eyes and felt she could have been looking at herself at one time. "Did they also tell you that I believe he had every intention of doing exactly that?"

Cait did not flinch from the warning explicit in Charity's tone and eyes. "Yes."

She was going to risk it, Charity knew. She was going to put her life at risk. Which was, admittedly, the way it should be. In Cait's situation.

With the brutal honesty that had always served her well, Charity readily admitted she no longer possessed that do-or-die drive. It wasn't that she was afraid to die; it was just that she'd be leaving too much behind to make the choice acceptable. Which was why she never, not for a single moment, missed her former life in the fast lane.

She sighed, took a sip of her cooling coffee and made her decision. Although reliving those days was not her favorite way to pass the time, she'd do it. If it would help save any woman the terror she'd experienced.

"It's about control," she said after a long pause. She stood up and took her jacket down from a wooden hook on the wall. "Do you mind if we walk while we talk? I usually patrol the cove about now."

Cait suspected Charity's sudden need for exercise had less to do with patrolling the waterfront than it did with a desire to work off some of the nervous energy thinking about the rapist had caused to build up inside her.

She stood up as well. "Let's go."

They walked for nearly two hours, Charity talking nonstop, pausing only to answer the few questions Cait quietly interjected. She told her everything—about the way he'd obviously stalked her for days before making his move, about the stench of the whiskey on his breath when he dragged her beneath that pier, about the feel of his fist slamming into her face, shattering her cheekbone, and most terrifyingly, about the belief that she was about to die.

"Does your husband know about all this?" Cait asked.

"No." Charity shook her head. "Oh, he knows I went undercover. And he knows that I caught the scumbag. But I don't think he truly comprehends how it went down. Which is probably just as well."

Although Starbuck accepted her career choice intellectually, she knew there were still times—such as last Saturday night when she'd had to break up yet another brawl at The Stewed Clam—that he worried about her safety.

"Doesn't he like you being a cop?"

Charity's smile returned. "That's a loaded question. If I say yes, I'm not exactly being honest. But if I say no, you'll think Starbuck's just another chauvinist who wants to keep females barefoot and pregnant."

Speaking of pregnant . . . Her smile warmed as she remembered how thrilled her husband had been when she informed him that he was going to be a father again.

"I know," she said, "why don't you come to dinner tonight? Starbuck's making lasagna and he always makes enough to feed the Italian army."

"Your husband cooks?"

Charity laughed at that, a rich, bubbling sound that wiped away the gloom created by their earlier conversation. "It's one of the reasons I married him."

Cait watched the sheriff's eyes turn to a dazzling sapphire. "But not the only reason," she guessed.

"No." A warm, intimate heat rose in Charity's eyes, creating another little stir of envy deep inside Cait. "Starbuck is definitely one of a kind. . . .

"Oh, and of course your friend is invited, too," she tacked on, proving to Cait that the small-town gossip line was working just fine.

9

ALTHOUGH HAVING DINNER with the town police chief's family, including her brother and sister-in-law, was not the way Sloan would have preferred to spend the evening, he found he enjoyed himself immensely.

Charity reminded him a great deal of Cait, with one obvious difference. Where Cait struggled to guard her emotions, Charity was an open book. Her love for her family—in particularly her husband and little boy—was more than obvious.

When he inadvertently glimpsed the couple exchanging a long, clandestine kiss in the kitchen, jealousy punched Sloan in the gut.

After dinner, the women put the two children—Prescott Dylan Valderian and Julianna's ten-month old daughter, Rachel Celeste Prescott, named after her two grandmothers—to bed. The men loaded the dishwasher, then went into the living room. "It's difficult, isn't it?" Starbuck surprised Sloan by asking suddenly. "Watching her strap on a side-arm every morning."

Sloan opened his mouth to explain that he'd yet to have the pleasure of waking up with Cait, then decided if he had his way, after tonight that would no longer be the case.

"I worry about her," he said instead. "And the idea of her taking on this case . . ."

His voice drifted off. Silence pooled around them. Sloan cursed and frowned into the crackling fire. Though the days carried the promise of spring, nights were still chilly on the island.

"Cait seems pretty capable," Dylan suggested helpfully.

"Cait's a damn good cop," Sloan agreed gruffly. Accustomed to researching his scripts in detail, he hadn't hesitated to ask a friend in the department to pull her jacket. All her superiors, including the commander of the Vice Squad detail had written glowingly of her intelligence and dedication. "But she's not Superwoman."

Starbuck gave the screenwriter a probing look as he sipped his brandy. Sloan Wyndham looked as if he'd been poleaxed. Starbuck knew the feeling. Intimately.

"When I first met Charity, I did not believe women should be peace officers," he revealed, smiling as he thought back to those early days.

"Later, even though I came to realize that her need to help people is a very strong part of why I fell in love with her in the first place, and although I am the first to acknowledge that my wife is very good at what she does, I must admit that there are still times when I am appalled at her willingness to put herself in harm's way.

"I also cannot deny that I'm very relieved she is no longer working in the city." Especially now that she was carrying his child, Starbuck mused.

"That makes two of us," Dylan allowed. He'd worried about his twin sister the entire time she'd been in California. "But, you may as well get used to it, Sloan," he advised. "Because I have the distinct impression that the lady has no intention of turning in her badge anytime soon."

"And believe me," Starbuck added encouragingly, "there are far worse things than being in love with a dedicated, warmhearted woman determined to preserve and protect her little corner of the world."

Love? Sloan wanted Cait with a desperation that bordered on obsession. She'd taken over his mind, his body, and yes, dammit, a part of his heart that had always remained off limits. But *love?*

While he was not yet prepared to admit, even to himself, that he was falling in love with Cait Carrigan, Sloan wouldn't bet against it, either.

Upstairs, as she watched Julianna lovingly tuck little Rachel Celeste between the sheets, Cait felt something soft and alien stir deep inside her.

Since it was getting late and a storm was threatening, it had been decided that Julianna and Dylan's daughter would spend the night here, rather than have to go out in the icy rain.

So now, as the little girl, who looked so much like her mother, with her pale blond hair and calm gray eyes, dutifully pressed her wet rosebud lips against Cait's cheek in a good-night kiss, Cait recognized the twinge as a quickening of her biological clock. That's all it was, she assured herself.

Understanding that this unbidden rush of warm emotion toward a child she'd just met was born from some primal instinct designed to perpetuate the species made it easier to accept.

Cait reminded herself that she did not have to succumb to strange maternal urges. She was, after all, a modern career woman. And the world certainly had more than enough people without her being expected to contribute to the population.

"Poor Sloan," Charity murmured as she shut the door to the bedroom. "He's having trouble with all this, isn't he?"

Although, as if by mutual unspoken agreement, no one at the table had mentioned the Surfer Rapist, the reason for Cait's trip to Maine had remained with them all during dinner—the elephant in the dining room no one dared to mention.

"He's not exactly wild about the idea," Cait agreed.

"That's not so surprising, really, is it?" Julianna said in her usual calm, logical voice. "Wouldn't you feel conflicted if you found yourself falling in love with a man who risked his life every time he went off to work?"

"If it was what he wanted to do . . ." Julianna's words belatedly sank in. "Sloan isn't in love with me."

"Of course he is," both women said in unison.

"You're probably too close to see it," Charity advised.

"*He* may not even know it yet," Julianna tacked on helpfully.

"But it's obvious that the guy's fallen hard, Cait. And it's just as obvious that he's worried to death about losing you."

"The same way Starbuck worries whenever he allows himself to think about the risks Charity takes," Julianna said.

"He seemed to handle yesterday's bar brawl story admirably enough," Cait argued.

"Starbuck's come a long way," Charity agreed, mindful of a time when her husband, in a misguided attempt to rescue her, had drawn her ire by interfering in just such a situation. "But there are still too many times when he's overprotective, even though he understands that I'm an intelligent, independent woman."

"My brother is very proud of Charity," Julianna said. "As he should be."

"But give him his druthers and he'd probably keep me safe in bed until the baby's born." Charity grinned and pressed her hand against her stomach.

Cait's gaze followed the unconsciously protective movement. Another jolt of envy, harder than the earlier one, but just as unbidden, and every bit as unwelcome, rocked her.

"The thing is," Charity, cheerfully oblivious to Cait's shattering response, continued with a smile, "I understand that Starbuck's sometimes frustrating behavior is his way of telling me that he loves me."

"Like Sloan loves you," Julianna finished up.

No. Cait still couldn't believe it. Lust, hunger, desire. Even need. There were so many words for what Sloan was feeling toward her. For what she was feeling toward him.

But it wasn't love. It couldn't be.

The lobby of The Gaslight Inn proved to be even more of a treasure trove of Victorian memorabilia than Cait had been aware of last night. The lushly furnished three-story white clapboard house was overflowing with innumerable curios and ornaments. Papier-mâché trays, porcelain-faced dolls, mother-of-pearl boxes, and miniature floral arrangements displayed beneath glass domes were only a few of the items seemingly covering every flat surface.

"This really is exquisite," Cait breathed.

Sloan decided, for discretion's sake, not to mention that the lacy clutter had him feeling vaguely claustrophobic. "She's got a lot of stuff," he agreed.

His tone revealed his lack of appreciation. "Let me guess. You hate antiques."

"I don't hate them."

He shrugged, thinking back on those days of living with whatever broken stuff his parents could scrounge up at the Salvation Army Thrift Stores. He'd always vowed that when he grew up and became rich and famous, he wasn't going to have to put up with anyone's cast-off things ever again. "I just don't understand why people think it's such a big deal to own some old termite-infested, secondhand table when factories are turning out new ones by the hundreds."

"That's just the point." Cait paused to admire the intricate carving on the back of a horsehair-covered sofa. "It's easy to find cookie-cutter furniture. Pieces like this are one of a kind."

The particular sofa she was stroking looked uncomfortable as hell. Sloan tried to imagine making love on it and decided it wasn't all that surprising that the Victorians had been sexually frustrated.

"Probably because most people had the sense to throw the things away when assembly lines started turning out practical, comfortable designs."

Understanding that not everyone shared her appreciation for the past, Cait merely shrugged. "Different strokes," she murmured. She glanced down at the window, where the rain was streaking down the glass. "I was going to suggest a walk on the beach, but—"

"I was going to suggest a nightcap."

"That sounds nice."

When she started to sit down on the sofa, Sloan decided it was time to move things along. "In my room."

"Oh."

She paused, looked first down at the hard horsehair cushion, then up at Sloan, who didn't even attempt to hide his longing for her. Even knowing that what she was about to do was a mistake, realizing that she was on the brink of complicating things terribly, Cait held out her hand.

"That sounds even better."

Neither spoke as they climbed the stairs. There was no need. For once, they were in total agreement.

Sloan paused outside his door, drew her into his arms and kissed her. A slow, intimate, knee-weakening kiss that promised many more to come.

Cait waited as he unlocked the door. She smiled, a soft, secret womanly smile as he drew her inside. Someone, undoubtedly the innkeeper, had laid a fire in the huge stone fireplace. When Cait viewed the high bed draped in gauze curtains that took up most of the room, her eyes widened.

"It's magnificent," she breathed.

"It's also too damn big for one person," he muttered as he lit the fire. He'd nearly gone crazy last night, thinking of Cait on the other side of the wall, imagining all the things he wanted to do with her in this ridiculously ornate bed.

He framed her exquisite face between his palms and looked down into her soft, emerald eyes. "This is going to change things."

The way he was looking at her, as if he could see all the way to her soul, made her feel both reckless and safe at the same time. She could feel her blood begin to pump in places aching for his touch. She was trembling. It both excited and unnerved her.

"Yes."

He brushed his lips against hers. "Once isn't going to be enough."

Cait parted her lips on a soft intake of breath. "I certainly hope not," she murmured against his mouth.

"Do you have any idea," he asked, his voice a husky rasp of sound, "how long I've been waiting to be with you like this?"

She looked up at him, a faint regret clouding her wide green eyes. "All of a week?"

Sloan experienced a masculine burst of relief that she was obviously unaccustomed to permitting such intimacy this soon in a relationship.

"Longer." He lowered his mouth to hers again. Her lips were sweet and soft and oh, so incredibly giving. "Years." The kiss grew deeper, staying tender even as it grew more and more intimate. "Forever."

Cait reminded herself that Sloan was a writer, that such weakening words came easily to him. Yet for some reason she would think about later, when her blood had cooled and the mists had blown away from her mind, she chose to believe him.

On some distant level, she realized that tomorrow there would be consequences. But thank God, tomorrow was a very long time away.

For a man who professed to want her desperately, Sloan seemed in no hurry to progress to the next step. Instead, he continued to kiss her slowly, deeply, dreamily.

Anticipation was making her nerves hum. "Sloan..." When those clever lips skimmed up the side of her face to linger at her temple, she caught his face between her palms and brought his mouth back to hers. "Please." Her knees were shaking, her heart was pounding, and she didn't know how much longer she could stand this tender torment. It seemed he intended to kiss her endlessly. "Make love to me."

He wondered if she knew exactly how accurate that soft plea was. Wondered if she realized that love had far more to do with what was about to happen between them than sex.

He slipped his hands beneath her sweater and felt her tremble, which sent a sense of power streaking through him. Cait Carrigan, he knew all too well, was not a woman to tremble for any man. But she was trembling for him.

"With," he corrected huskily as he eased the sweater over her shoulders, her head. To his surprise, rather than the brazen silk and satin he'd expected, she was wearing a tight-fitting, ribbed cotton top cut off at her midriff.

What was even more surprising was that he'd never known exactly how sexy plain white underwear could be.

"With?" she echoed. Heat that had nothing to do with the crackling fire across the room, but everything to do with the flare of passion in his eyes, seemed to scorch her flesh, liquefying her bones.

"I don't want to make love *to* you, Cait," he clarified as he began to unbutton the brief, tight-fitting top. When his knuckles brushed against the crest of her breast, she drew in a deep, shuddering breath. "I want to make love *with* you."

Dear Lord, that was what she wanted, too. As he continued to undress her, Cait's murmurs urged him to hurry. But although it took a herculean effort on his part, Sloan continued to take his time, undressing her piece by piece, as if unwrapping the most precious of gifts, treating each bit of newly exposed flesh to a pleasure that Cait had no words to describe.

By the time he'd dispensed with his clothes and finally lowered her to the wide soft feather bed, she'd decided that not even sublime came close.

"You are so soft." His hands glided over flesh that gleamed like marble in the flickering firelight. "So sweet." His lips grazed her heated flesh from her forehead to her toes, discovering hidden secrets until she was writhing on the hot sheets in mindless ecstasy.

He combed his fingers through the fiery curls between her smooth long legs, then, as she arched upward toward his hand in a mute plea, he slipped his fingers between those slick, excruciatingly sensitive pink lips. His stroking, caressing touch brought her deftly and quickly to a peak that left Cait stunned and gasping for breath.

"So perfect." And, he thought with a burst of male possessiveness mingled with love, she was his. All his. Although he'd never expected it, never believed himself capable of falling in love, Sloan felt the emotion flowing through him, as strong as a river, as wide and endless as the sea.

In her open gaze he could see twin reflections of the orange and blue fire. And an emotion he could only hope was love.

Her damp flesh gleamed like pearls in the firelight, her hair was a wild, sensuous witch's tangle of red and copper and gold, her green eyes were wide and bold and daring and her lips—oh, God, those sweet, succulent lips—were full and parted.

He braced himself over her. "There'll be no going back," he warned, his voice roughened by his overwhelming, greedy hunger. "After tonight, you're my woman, Cait."

At any other time, in any other place, Cait would have protested such a declaration of male possessiveness. But her own need was too great. Her own hunger too strong.

"Yours." She raked her hands through his hair and dragged his mouth to hers, praying the rest of his body would follow.

It did.

He surged into her, slick hot flesh to hot flesh, steel into silk, causing her body to arch in stunned, mindless pleasure. He pressed her deeper and deeper into the mattress, his face buried in her fragrant hair. Her hands ran heatedly, restlessly, up and down his back, her short nails scraping his skin. Neither noticed as he drove them both, thrust for thrust, toward the final crest. Cait's legs tightened around his waist, her body, poised on a death-defying peak, stiffened. When he plunged again, deeper than she could have ever imagined possible, she cried out his name as she went tumbling headlong over the edge.

Sloan felt the convulsions ricocheting from deep within her amazingly responsive body, milking him to his own explosive release.

THEY WERE LYING in a tangle of arms and legs. The fire was burning down, but Sloan lacked both energy and inclination to get up and restoke the flames.

"Tell me again," he said as he arranged her love-tousled hair over her breasts. The brush of his fingertips caused a slight tremor that assured him that her desire, while temporarily sated, still lingered warmly beneath the surface.

"Tell you what?"

Her eyes were closed. The long cross-country trip, her sleepless night, the horrors that Charity had revealed about the Surfer Rapist, not to mention Sloan's tumultuous lovemaking, had all conspired to exhaust her. Physically and mentally drained, she was floating on the edge of sleep.

"That you're mine."

His husky implication caused her eyes to fly open and sent shock waves reverberating through her. It took nearly a full minute before she could speak.

"Sloan . . ." She couldn't hide her distress. It shimmered in her ragged voice, swirled in her eyes. "We were making love."

Surely he didn't intend to hold her to something said in the throes of passion. Besides, it was all his fault for making her unable to think straight in the first place.

"Exactly." He ran his hand down her hair, before cupping her chin and holding her unsettled gaze to his. "You can't deny that what we shared wasn't any routine, run-of-the-mill sex."

"No, but—"

"I love you, Cait."

"That's impossible."

"Why?"

"Because you don't even know me."

"I know enough to understand that what I feel for you is a helluva lot more than physical. I know I've never felt this way about any other woman in my life. I know I want to spend the rest of my life making love with you.

"And most of all—" he bent his head and kissed her downturned lips "—I want to make babies with you. A passel of smart-mouthed, gorgeous redheaded kids with tempers just like their mother."

Sloan Wyndham might be a brilliant writer and director. But he was obviously crazy.

So what else was new? Cait wondered. Most of her parents' friends were more than a little off center as well.

As wrong as she knew he was, Cait found herself unwilling to argue after their incredible lovemaking. "I don't know what to say."

He reached out and uncurled her fingers from the fist they'd unconsciously tightened into.

"You don't have to say anything." He lifted their joined hands and without taking his eyes from hers, brushed his lips against her knuckles, causing her pulse to jump. "I just thought it only fair that you know how I felt. So you could get used to the idea."

When he kissed her again, on her frowning lips, Cait told herself it was time to leave. Now. While she still could. "I should get back to my room."

His teeth nipped gently, tantalizingly at her chin. "Don't tell me you'd be so cruel as to make me spend another night all alone in this ridiculously romantic bed?"

"It's not a ridiculous bed." He moved on to her earlobe, creating a renewed stir of desire.

"Not for lovers. But it's not exactly the kind of bed a man would choose to sleep in all by himself."

Although the fire had died down, a silvery light from a full moon outside the window streamed through the white lace curtains, draping the room in shadows while making her skin gleam like starshine.

Gazing down at her, Sloan wondered, as he had for days, what exactly it was about Cait that had so completely captured both his mind and his heart. She was stunningly beautiful, granted. But he'd been living in California for nearly a decade and had known other women equally as lovely. She was intelligent. But so was her friend Blythe, and although he admired Blythe Fielding's brains, tenacity and talent, and yes, her sultry, sexy dark looks, he certainly hadn't found himself wanting to lick every inch of the actress's fragrant skin the moment he'd met her.

Like he'd wanted to do with Cait. And like he was wanting to do again.

"Don't leave me, sweet Cait." Love, more than desire, had him pressing his lips against her bare shoulder. "Not tonight." *Not ever* he thought, but had enough sense, after her less than enthusiastic response to his spontaneous declaration of love, not to say.

His hands cupped her breasts as his lips skimmed hotly along her shoulder blades. He was jumbling her senses all over again.

"All right," she said on a soft sigh of surrender. "You win, Sloan." She turned in his arms and lifted her face to his. "I'll stay the night."

Even as Cait warned herself that tomorrow morning she would have to find some way to convince Sloan that this stolen night together was all they were going to have, all they *could* have, Sloan was vowing to convince her that if she'd only allow herself to trust him, they could both end up winners.

SHE'D MADE A fatal mistake. The thought reverberated in Cait's mind, ricocheting around like bullets. During the long, love-filled night in Sloan's bed, she'd shared more passion than she'd experienced in a lifetime. But now, in the clear bright light of a new Maine morning, she knew that by letting her guard down, she'd opened herself up to a vast amount of heartache.

She didn't want to love him. She didn't want to believe that he could possibly love her. Love was fleeting. Transitory. Love hurt.

It did not take a mind reader to sense the change in Cait once the sun had risen over the rocky east shore of Castle Mountain. Even as she lay in his arms, Sloan could feel her retreating back behind emotional parapets she'd spent a lifetime constructing.

"Regrets so soon?" he murmured against her temple.

When he ran his palm from her shoulder to her hip, Cait was amazed that after the incredible night they'd shared, it only took a touch of his hand to create that now familiar heat.

"Of course not," she lied quietly.

Even as he told himself not to push, impatience had him needing to know. "But something's wrong."

She sighed and closed her eyes. "I enjoyed last night, Sloan."

"So did I." He pressed his lips against her fragrant hair. "More than I could have imagined."

"I know the feeling." Sloan waited for the other shoe to drop. He did not have to wait long.

"The thing is," she continued haltingly, "I think we need to keep it in perspective."

"In perspective?" If she hadn't been so wrapped up in her own tumultuous feelings, she would have heard the terse warning sound in his tone.

She opened her eyes and found herself looking directly into his. "I'll admit that the chemistry between us has been amazingly strong from the beginning. Add to that the fact that we're both single, unattached adults and it was probably inevitable that we'd end up in bed together."

He could hear this one coming. Having never been rejected by a woman, Sloan realized that if he'd given the matter any thought at all, which he never had, he might have expected a sting to the ego. What he could never have foreseen was this icy, overwhelming fear.

"Sounds reasonable to me."

"But now that it's happened, I think the best thing for us to do is to get on with our own lives."

Sloan had never thought of himself as a violent man. But at this moment, he wanted to grab hold of her shoulders and shake some sense into that beautiful head. He wanted to tie her to the gauze-draped bedposts and keep her hostage, making love to her over and over again until she realized there would be no getting on with their individual lives.

"Are you saying," he asked slowly, carefully, "that you don't want me to do this ever again?" He cupped her breast, thinking, as he had so many times last night, how perfectly the softly rounded flesh fit in his hand. "Or this?" His mouth covered hers in a swift swoop; his tongue thrust into the dark recesses as his hand moved over her rib cage, her stomach, then lower still, where warm moisture pooled in response to his deep kiss and stroking hand.

"Dammit, Sloan—" she protested, even as her mutinous body arched like a bow, seeking relief.

Despite a flash fire temper she'd admittedly worked hard to control, she'd always been proud of her self-control. Until she'd met a man who, with a devastating smile, a hot look, or a single touch, could shatter such hard won control.

"I love you, Cait." His fingers slipped into her with a silky ease. His thumb caressed the pink nub that was ultrasensitive after the long night of lovemaking. "And I'm going to make love to you whenever and wherever I get the opportunity."

This was no mere Hollywood screenwriter. Sloan Wyndham was obviously a sorcerer, dabbling in black magic. He was doing it to her all over again, with his wicked touch and dark taste. Clouds drifted over Cait's mind. She couldn't think. All she could do was feel.

Her warm flesh glowed. Her eyes drifted shut. Sloan watched her fly. Higher and higher. And then, he held her as she came floating back to earth.

It was a long time before either of them spoke. Cait lay in his arms, confused and conflicted, until she was certain her quaking legs could hold her upright. Then, without a word, she left his bed. And his room. Moments later, he heard the rumble of ancient pipes and realized she was taking a shower.

With a muttered curse, Sloan crossed his arms behind his head and stared up at the ceiling, trying to keep from opening that adjoining door and taking her beneath the pulsating stream of warm water.

She might be able to wash away the physical evidence of their lovemaking, Sloan thought. But she couldn't wash away the truth—that as unlikely as he would have thought it only a week ago, he and Cait Carrigan were destined to be together.

Sloan was not all that surprised when Cait continued the silent treatment over breakfast. Nor did she speak during the brief plane ride to the mainland.

They were sitting side by side in the Bangor terminal, awaiting the boarding call for the flight to Boston when she suddenly turned to him.

"When we get back to L.A., I have an important job to do. I can't allow myself to be distracted."

Once again he resented being referred to as a distraction. Once again he held his tongue. Because, although he wanted her to think of only him, Sloan realized that to distract her now, while she was attempting to apprehend a murderous psychopath, could end up getting her killed.

"Point taken." He reached out and took her hand, the gesture more friendly than seductive. "Although I'm not going to change the way I feel, I promise not to push, Cait. Until that creep is back behind bars where he belongs."

Cait didn't miss the fact that Sloan left open the possibility of a renewed relationship after her undercover assignment was completed. But, still unable to believe that his alleged feelings for her would last that long, she allowed herself to feel relieved.

"Thank you." She managed a smile.

As he watched the warmth of that smile slowly turn her eyes to a brilliant emerald, Sloan prayed that the case of the escaped Surfer Rapist would be brought to a quick and safe—for Cait—end.

And then, he vowed, he had every intention of making the luscious Cait Carrigan his. Forever.

Later, as the jet raced the sun across the country, Sloan considered the irony of his situation—that he, the off-spring of an escaped murderer and a rebellious, runaway Philadelphia socialite was going to marry a cop.

He was going to have to tell Cait the truth, he mused as he sipped a Scotch and stared down at the vast Nebraska plains. If his mother wasn't still alive, locked in the misty labyrinth of her own mind in that overpriced, spalike funny farm, he might have been able to keep his lifelong secret.

But Sloan knew that he couldn't have done it.

He loved Cait. And that being the case, he owed her the truth of exactly who—and what—he was.

Ancient dreads rose unbidden like specters, darkening his mood and making Sloan wonder if Fate was about to teach him, yet again, exactly how ephemeral happiness could be.

10

DREADING WHAT SHE KNEW would be a confrontation, Blythe called Alan at his home from her dressing room. She'd already been unable to meet his plane at the airport; now, thanks to continued problems on the set, she wasn't going to be able to make his all-important dinner.

"Sturgess here," the male voice on the other end answered abruptly.

"Hello, Alan," she began carefully, "it's Blythe."

"Where are you?" he demanded.

"I'm afraid I'm still at the studio."

"The studio? What are you doing there?"

She could imagine his dark brows crawling up his patrician forehead. A typical surgeon, Alan Sturgess lived his life in warp drive. He was always on his way to someplace or from someplace, and inevitably he was in a hurry. He was punctual to a fault and had little patience with slackers.

"It's a long story."

"Blythe, we're already overdue. Even if we were to leave here right now, we'd still miss most of the cocktail hour."

"I realize that, Alan. But I got tied up. We've been having the worst day. First, the rain machine wouldn't work, then Martin found out that you could see right through my underpants when I got wet—"

"What!"

At least she'd momentarily sidetracked him, Blythe considered. "Don't worry, we fixed it," she said quickly. "The wardrobe mistress sewed in an extra panel. She told me it's what they do with all those athletes on those cotton brief commercials."

"Isn't that a useful piece of information. And to think that there are actually people who fail to take the movie business seriously."

And unfortunately, Blythe thought, she was engaged to one of them. "There's no need to be sarcastic, Alan," she said quietly. Firmly. "I understand that you're disappointed, but—"

"Disappointed doesn't begin to cover it. You knew how important this dinner was to me, Blythe."

Yes, of course she did. "I know, darling." Blythe wearily rubbed the back of her neck and rotated her shoulders, attempting to work out the knots caused by the stress of the overly hectic and frustratingly long day.

"But I certainly didn't plan for all these problems," she said, a hint of irritation creeping into her tone as well. "And although I realize that my work isn't nearly as important as a tummy tuck or face-lift on some aging star or socialite, I happen to take it very seriously." There was a moment of silence.

"You don't sound yourself tonight," he said finally, obviously surprised by her uncharacteristic sarcasm. "Are you all right, Blythe?"

She sighed. "I'm just tired. And wet. And cold."

"You're trying to do too much," he said with obvious concern, reminding Blythe that he had her own best interests at heart. "What with making this film while trying to get your own project off the ground, not to mention planning a wedding, you're burning the candle at both ends."

"Probably," she agreed. "But I don't really have any choice."

"I warned you that forming your own production company would be a mistake."

"It's not a mistake. I've been acting since I was three years old, Alan. It's time I had some artistic control."

"You could always retire," he suggested, not for the first time since they'd decided to get married. "As you said, darling, you've been working since you were a child. Perhaps it's time you took a break."

They'd had this discussion before. She had tried to explain about her need to work, to which he'd countered that as the Chief of Staff's wife, she would have plenty to do to keep her busy.

What he couldn't seem to understand was that making movies was in her blood. She could no more envision giving it up—especially to host afternoon teas for other doctors' wives—than she could imagine giving up breathing.

"Alan—"

"I know," he said, "I'm pushing again." She could hear his resigned sigh over the wires. "But if you weren't spending all the hours you're supposed to be sleeping trying to research some sixty-year-old Hollywood murder mystery, you wouldn't be so worn out at the end of your day, darling."

He couldn't understand her obsession with Alexandra Romanov's murder. Truthfully, Blythe didn't really understand it herself. All she knew was that since she'd first heard the story, she'd not been able to put it out of her mind.

"Not everyone has your energy, dear." Her voice softened to that of a woman coaxing a man to reason. "But I understand how important this evening is to you, and I'm truly sorry I'm going to have to disappoint you again.

"All I can say is that I promise things will get better as soon as this picture wraps. And I hope you won't mind too much attending without me."

"Of course I'll mind not getting a chance to be with you." His own tone had softened as well. It was deep and warm and radiated with that inimitable self-confidence she imagined his patients found vastly reassuring. "You're wonderful company, Blythe, darling. Not to mention being a marvelous asset."

Thinking that he made her sound like one of the thoroughbreds he'd invested in as a tax shelter, Blythe didn't answer.

"And since everyone knows that Menninger prefers his staff to be happily married," Alan continued, "it certainly wouldn't have hurt to remind everyone that we're tying the knot. But, I'll understand if you don't feel up to socializing."

Blythe fought down the unbidden surge of resentment that he'd actually be willing to use their upcoming marriage to further his career. Exhausted as she was, she'd probably misinterpreted his words. Alan might not admire her choice in careers, but she'd never harbored a single doubt that he loved her. And only wanted the best for her.

"Thank you, Alan."

"May I offer another suggestion?"

"What?"

"Why don't I drop by after dinner? That way we can still spend some quality time together."

He was the only man Blythe knew who actually used that clichéd term in conversation. But he was also intelligent, and handsome, and he loved her enough to put up with her impossible schedule.

"I'm sorry, Alan," she said. "But I'm afraid any time spent with me tonight would be a total waste."

There was a moment of disappointed silence.

"You need to take better care of yourself. Making yourself ill won't get your project produced."

He was right on the money about that, Blythe admitted. "I promise to go to bed the minute I get home."

"You know," he suggested offhandedly, "Peter Oliver just returned from Maui with his new wife. He says the islands are an ideal spot for a honeymoon."

Blythe dragged a hand through her hair. "Alan—"

"We have to pick a spot, Blythe. The wedding's in less than a week and you still haven't let me make any reservations."

"I know." She opened her mouth to explain that she'd had too much on her mind to even think about a honeymoon, then realized that all she'd be doing would be making his point for him.

"Why can't we just stay home?" she suggested instead. "We can turn off the phones, and—"

"If I don't get you away from here, I'll end up sharing you with directors, writers and Lord knows what other creative types.

"Meanwhile," he said when she didn't answer, letting her off the hook for now, "you're probably right about tonight. Why don't you take a long hot bath? And open one of those pleasant bottles of cabernet sauvignon we bought last month at Temecula. A little wine will relax you."

A little wine would put her out like a light, Blythe decided. "That's a good idea," she said. "Have a good time at the party. Please give my apologies to Dr. and Mrs. Menninger. And good luck."

"Without you at my side, I'll need all the luck I can get. Good night, darling. Sleep well."

"Good night," she repeated softly.

She replaced the receiver to the cradle, sighed, then dragged herself back to the set.

Two days later, the film that she'd seemed destined to spend the rest of her life working on, finally wrapped. Now that the project had been handed over to the postproduction team, Blythe was free to turn at least some of her attention to her upcoming wedding.

The first item of business, she decided, was the dress. Alan had asked about it again during their nightly phone call last night and, unwilling to admit she hadn't even found time to go shopping, Blythe had hedged, murmuring something about wanting it to be a surprise.

Knowing that Cait had returned from Maine, Blythe called her at her apartment. Since she wasn't due at police headquarters until later that afternoon, Cait had immediately agreed to accompany Blythe on the shopping trip she'd put off for far too long.

"The problem is," Cait complained to Blythe as she locked her apartment door behind her, shouting to be heard over the bagpipe rendition of "Viva Las Vegas" coming from the apartment downstairs, "there are miles of coastline for the creep to choose from. And millions of women." She shook her head with disgust. "It's a logistical nightmare, getting him to zero in on me."

Cait had filled Blythe in on some of what Charity had revealed. And although she suspected there was a great deal more that her friend wasn't telling her, Blythe had heard enough to be even more worried than when she'd first learned of the plan.

"Why don't you just call a press conference?" Blythe suggested dryly. "And announce you're available?"

To Blythe's amazement, Cait didn't immediately reject her suggestion, which had been part sarcasm, part jest. "You know," Cait said thoughtfully as they left the building, "that's not such a bad idea."

"I was only kidding," Blythe said, immediately alarmed by the spark of interest in Cait's eyes.

Cait was still thinking about Blythe's impulsive suggestion twenty minutes later as she sipped a cappuccino at the oak bar of a trendy Rodeo Drive boutique while the accommodating saleswoman displayed the gowns she'd selected after receiving Blythe's telephone call this morning.

Blythe appeared to be trying to set a world record for shopping for wedding apparel, Cait considered, as she watched her friend reject one exquisite gown after another.

Finally, just when the saleswoman's accommodating smile had begun to slip a notch, Blythe said, "I'll take that one."

The dress was simple by Rodeo Drive standards—a sleek, off-the-shoulder, short sleeved ivory crepe tunic over a long slender skirt. It was extremely elegant, Cait thought, although she couldn't help picturing Blythe in something more romantic. More bridelike. Her second thought was that Blythe had obviously chosen something her excruciatingly stuffy bridegroom would approve.

"Aren't you even going to try it on?" she asked.

"There's no need." Blythe handed over her American Express card. "It's my size, it'll fit. Besides, you're due at the station soon."

Although they had another two hours before Cait was expected to join the other members of the task force, she knew better than to argue when Blythe had made up her mind. Even having no plans to marry herself, Cait nevertheless thought the purchase of a wedding dress should be a more special occasion than Blythe was making it.

"I'm going to make you mad again," she warned Blythe as they returned to Bachelor Arms. "But I need you to explain to me, one more time, why you're marrying Alan."

"Because I love him, of course," Blythe responded promptly.

"What about lust?"

Blythe slanted her a look, wondering if the out-of-the-blue question had anything to do with Sloan accompanying Cait on her trip to Maine. "What about it?"

"Do you lust for him?"

If the question had come from anyone else, Blythe would have promptly told them it was none of their business. But because she and Cait had been friends for so long, as she stopped for a red light at Rodeo and Sunset, Blythe answered honestly.

"Lust is overrated. Besides, it doesn't last." She tapped her fingers on the steering wheel as she waited for the light to turn green. "I respect Alan. I'm fond of him. He'll be an excellent companion."

"Sounds like you should be shopping for a golden retriever instead of a wedding dress."

"That's not nice. I truly love Alan. Life isn't all razzle dazzle excitement like in the movies. And the one thing you and I have in common is that neither one of us wants to marry anyone in the movie business."

The light turned green again, allowing Blythe to turn. "You know as well as I do that the industry is like a roller coaster, and even the best marriages have enough ups and downs without adding professional jealousy.

"Besides, with fifty percent of marriages failing—and even worse odds in this town—I feel safe marrying Alan." Blythe smiled. "I can easily see us celebrating our fiftieth anniversary."

Personally, Cait thought fifty years with Alan Sturgess would be the equivalent of doing hard time. "Why get married at all?"

"Because I want children," Blythe said without hesitation. "I'm also old-fashioned enough to believe that when possible, two parents are better than one. And Alan will make an excellent father."

If you considered Duvall's autocratic portrayal of fatherhood in *The Great Santini* to be a role model, Cait countered silently.

By the time Blythe pulled up in front of Bachelor Arms, Cait was already feeling sorry for the poor kids.

Later that evening, Cait was sitting in front of her television, wrapped up in an oversize purple terry cloth robe and eating her way through a pepperoni pizza, when someone began pounding on her door.

A glance through the peephole revealed Sloan. He was not smiling.

Suspecting she knew what had him so angry, she sighed and opened the door.

"What the hell do you think you're doing?" he demanded, marching into her living room as if he had every right to be there.

"Eating a pizza and watching a movie." She pointed at the red-and-white box atop the green marble-topped Victorian table. "Would you like a piece? There's enough for two."

"What I'd like is for you to explain what the hell that press conference was all about."

"Oh." She closed the door with another sigh. "Actually, that was Blythe's idea."

"Blythe? I can't believe it was her idea for you to put yourself at risk that way!"

"She may have been kidding," Cait allowed. "But I thought it was a good idea. So, obviously, did my superiors." She lifted her chin in that pugnacious gesture he recognized all too well. "I thought it went very well, actually."

Better than well. Realizing the need to alert innocent women who might fall victim to the serial rapist, the chief of police had called a press conference announcing the convict's escape. At Cait's suggestion, they'd staged the event on the Malibu pier. The chief had assured the people of Los

Angeles that the man would be quickly apprehended. In the meantime, he suggested women refrained from going to the beach alone.

On cue, just as he'd finished answering the questions and left the pier, Cait sauntered by in a bikini brief enough to capture any male's immediate attention. She was carrying a red-and-white surfboard that matched the polka dots on the minuscule suit. The press descended on her like sea gulls fighting over an abandoned french fry.

"Am I afraid?" she answered one of the television reporters. "Hell, no." She tossed her red hair over her shoulder with obvious feminine disdain. "I come to this beach every morning and every evening. There's no way I'm going to let some crazy pervert keep me from having fun."

That said, she waved to the assembled press and strolled out into the surf, where the television cameras from all the network affiliates and various independent stations filmed her paddling into the sunset-brightened surf.

"You put yourself out there like a piece of bait," Sloan objected. Having always considered himself adept with words, he knew he'd never be able to describe the mixture of fear and fury that had flooded over him while watching that news report.

"That's my job," she reminded him.

It was the same thing she'd already told him. The same thing Starbuck and Dylan had told him. The same thing he'd been trying to tell himself.

"I'm trying to understand why you feel you have to do this," he said. His expression was grim; brackets formed on either side of his lips. "But I'm not going to deny that I hate it."

Looking up at the emotions warring on Sloan's handsome face, Cait realized she was in deep, deep trouble. As if her heart had taken on a mind of its own, she was falling in love with him.

"I know it takes getting used to." She placed a hand against his rigid dark cheek and felt the muscle tense beneath her palm. "Would it make you feel any better to know that I'm going to have tons of backup?"

"Not really." What would make him feel better would be for her to give up this dangerous quest in the first place. But then she wouldn't be who she was, Sloan admitted. And he wouldn't have fallen so hard.

"Perhaps I can convince you that the operation is really a lot safer than it sounds." Her hand trailed down his face, along the side of his neck.

"I doubt that."

"I could try." Going up on her toes, she pressed her lips against his chin. "I can be very persuasive." She kissed the deep frown lines framing his firmly cut lips. "When I put my mind to it."

Feeling himself giving in, as he'd known all along he would, Sloan caught hold of her waist. "It might take some time," he warned.

"That's the same thing I was thinking." She linked her fingers around his neck and pressed the body he'd come to know so well against his. "Blythe and I went shopping today," she murmured against his neck.

"That's nice." Cupping her buttocks to lift her to his rising arousal, he didn't really focus on her seeming change in subject.

She could feel his sex stirring against her belly and had a sudden urge to drop to her knees and press her mouth against the denim placket of his jeans. An urge she resisted. For now.

"Blythe bought a wedding dress." She pressed closer. "I bought an extra toothbrush."

His hand slid between them to untie the voluminous robe. To his absolute delight she was wearing nothing beneath it. "Are you saying what I think you're saying?"

With a feminine smile, she backed away and shrugged the robe off her shoulders, where it fell to the floor around her feet. She stepped out of it and held out her hands. Her eyes gleamed with a gilt-edged invitation.

"I want you to spend the night with me, Sloan."

Forgetting that he'd been tempted to wring her lissome neck when he'd first arrived, Sloan scooped her up in his arms and carried her into the adjoining bedroom.

"Sweetheart, I thought you'd never ask."

IT WAS RAINING. The day had broken with dense gray skies and rain. A cold drizzle that seeped into the bones. Although Cait told herself that no serial rapist with any sense at all would be stalking a woman in weather like this, especially when sunny days were the norm in L.A., she couldn't take the chance that the one day she didn't stake out the beach would be the day he'd show up. So far, thank God, there'd been no reported rapes matching the description of the escapee's MO.

Since his victims had always been surfers—or girlfriends willing to wait patiently on the beach while the guys challenged the sea—the undercover plan was much the same as it had been when Charity apprehended the rapist the first time.

Unlike Charity, who, never having learned to surf, had played the role of a beach bunny, Cait, who'd spent her teenage years on the beaches up and down the southern California coast had chosen to go all the way.

Every day for the past five days, she'd joined the dawn patrol and the evening riders, deftly riding the undulating curls.

This evening the waves were ominous, rising like a thick wall that grew and grew into a massive swell that growled across Malibu's Third Point.

A former recreational surfer, it did not take Cait long to realize that she was in over her head, both literally and figuratively. After wiping out four straight times in a row, and almost being hit on the head by a piece of driftwood, she decided to call it quits.

After lashing her board on the rack atop her car, she returned to the beach to watch others more skillful or foolhardy than she brave the wild surf. With the exception of the undercover officers who jogged along the wet sand at the water's edge, blending in as typical California exercise fanatics, the beach was nearly deserted. The only other occupant was an elderly woman who, dressed in a bright flowered muumuu covered with a clear plastic raincoat, walked her ancient cocker spaniel as she had each morning and evening Cait had come to the beach.

Her teeth chattering from the chill, Cait wrapped a towel around her torso and stripped the wet suit from her body. Changing clothes on a public beach took practice. Her numb fingers almost dropped the towel.

As it slipped down her breasts, a voice from the radio secreted in her tote bag, said, "Nice touch, Carrigan. If that little peep show doesn't hook him, nothing will."

The male voice came from one of the squad's observers, who was standing on the cliff above, appearing to be just another tourist watching the action. Despite the seriousness of the situation, she could hear the repressed laughter in his tone.

"Go to hell, O'Hara," she muttered, yanking the towel back up again, tucking the end in more firmly, before pulling on a pair of baggy gray fleece sweat pants. Although not exactly the sexiest item of apparel in her closet, it was too cold for her bikini. Besides, rape was not about sex, but control.

After she finished dressing, Cait picked up her tote bag again and went strolling along the waterfront, as she had every day. When she reached the pier, she sat down on a wide flat rock and waited.

"I think we may as well call it a day," the voice said. "The guy isn't going to show. It's scheduled to clear up tomorrow morning. Maybe we'll have better luck then."

Cait certainly hoped so. She was beginning to feel as if she were living three separate lives. Early mornings she'd spend on the beach. Then, during the middle of the day, she'd help Blythe plan her wedding, although the conversation inevitably shifted away from the upcoming nuptials to the Alexandra Romanov project.

Then, as the sun set, she'd be back here, trolling for her rapist.

Nights were spent with Sloan. Although they made love with a frequency and a passion that continued to stun her, they also talked. To her amazement, Cait had found herself telling him about her childhood, about the game of musical mates her parents had played, about the continual parade of stepmothers and stepfathers and stepsisters and brothers.

Each night he'd manage, somehow, to draw more from her, including something she'd never even told Blythe. About one particular stepfather—who'd only lasted six weeks, fortunately—who'd possessed not only a roving eye, but roving hands as well.

She'd been thirteen when he'd cornered her in the kitchen and put his hands on her budding breasts and his tongue down her throat. Terrified and furious at the same time, she'd grabbed a nearby butcher knife and threatened to castrate him if he ever touched her again.

Apparently, he'd believed her. With good reason, Cait assured Sloan.

Recalling that story she'd tried so hard to forget had not been easy. Neither had telling it to Sloan. But with a tenderness that was so at odds with the steely strength beneath his handsome exterior, he'd held her in his arms and kissed away her tears. Afterward, he'd made love to her with something close to reverence that had made Cait weep all over again.

Her thoughts focused on Sloan, on how close they'd grown in such a short time, on how much she'd already come to count on him being in her life, Cait was only vaguely aware of the others leaving the beach.

She'd just realized that although he'd talk about politics, world events, sports, his work, or how things were progressing on Blythe's Alexandra project, he'd never—not once—shared any of his past with her.

For all Cait knew, he could have been a pod person, dropped suddenly onto the planet and into her life from outer space.

Without having realized it was happening, she'd invited him into the deepest, darkest, most intimate corners of her mind and soul. It was time—past time—for him to share.

"Beginning tonight," she vowed as she climbed the concrete stairs to the roadside parking lot.

Cait was already in her car, prepared to drive away, when she remembered that she'd left her tote bag, along with the radio, on the beach. Unwilling to blow her excellent record by being disciplined for losing expensive police property, she returned to the beach to retrieve it. Nearby, the elderly woman, apparently oblivious to the cold, was tossing a stick into the surf for her dog to retrieve.

The tide was coming in. The aged wood, covered with barnacles, creaked overhead. Beneath the pier it was dark and silent. And a little frightening.

Cait grabbed her tote and had just turned around when she felt someone come up behind her. She spun around and exhaled a huge sigh of relief when she viewed the old woman. The dog, she noted, on some distant level, was nowhere to be seen.

A vague intuitive uneasiness stirred. "Hi," she said.

The woman didn't answer. Goose bumps that had nothing to do with the chilly sea air rose on Cait's flesh.

She'd no sooner turned to leave when she was tackled from behind, thrown facedown into the water.

As strong hands yanked viciously at the waistband of her sweats, Cait began to fight.

For her life.

11

STUPID, stupid, stupid!

Furious at herself for having made such a rookie mistake, Cait turned on her attacker with a flash of white-hot rage. Kicking violently against the strong hands that were attempting to rip her sweatpants off her, she went for the eyes, managing instead to rake her nails down his face when he turned his head.

Blood spurted from the long claw marks. Cursing viciously, he curled the fingers of his right hand in a fist and hit her on the side of the face. Cait had not known that a punch could hurt so much. She saw stars, and then, for a moment, her vision blurred. Striking out blindly, her flailing hands grasped the pewter gray wig and jerked it off. It fell into the swirling water and went unnoticed.

Even as he struggled with the now wet sweatpants, the rapist continued to drag her further beneath the pier. Cait resisted with every atom of her strength. It crossed her mind that he might have a weapon—a knife, or even a gun—but then she remembered the police photos of the women he'd battered and remembered what Charity had told her about him seeming to enjoy the feel and sound of his fists shattering his victim's bones.

Reminding herself that was one thing she had in her favor, she continued landing punches wherever she could, on his face, his shoulders, his chest.

"I'm a cop, dammit!" she shouted against the roar of the tide.

He actually had the nerve to laugh at that. "You don't think I figured that out for myself?" he challenged. "Fool me once, shame on you."

He hit her again, a strong, full-powered blow that exploded against her jaw and caused the back of her head to slam against the wet sand. "Fool me twice, shame on me." Another blow, between the ribs, managed to suck the wind from her lungs. "So arrest me, why don't you?" he suggested evilly. Despite her best efforts to resist, he'd managed to yank the pants down to her knees. Even as she continued to struggle, through the haze of pain his fists were creating, Cait realized that he was trying to turn her over, to bury her face in the sand and surf. To suffocate her.

Relying on her Police Academy martial arts training, she slammed the side of her hand against his windpipe at the same time her heel managed to connect with his groin. A guttural roar bellowed out of him, making him sound like a wounded lion. He released her and curled up in a fetal ball, wheezing for live-saving air while clutching his wounded testicles.

Cait struggled to her feet, pulled up her sweatpants and ran on shaking legs for her tote bag. She'd just managed to get her pistol out when he managed to stand up as well.

At any other time, she might have thought about how silly he looked in that old-lady dress. But there was absolutely nothing funny about either her murderous assailant or the situation.

"Don't come any closer," she warned. She was standing in a two-legged stance, pistol gripped in both hands, just as she'd been taught. "It's over." Her chest was burning. Breathing was proving an effort, but she managed, with absolute concentration, to keep the gun steady. "You're under arrest."

At that he roared and lunged toward her again.

Cait pulled the trigger.

There was a thunderous explosion and a fire flash of light. Then only the soft sound of the wavelets washing against the cool pale sand and the creak of the wooden pier overhead.

SLOAN WAS IN Cait's kitchen, preparing paella when the squad car brought her home. One glance at her bruised face and he felt a rage so white-hot for the first time in his life he understood the term *crime of passion*. He also understood exactly how a reasonably sane person could commit murder.

"I'll kill the son of a bitch," he said, even as he enveloped her in his arms.

"She already took care of that," the uniformed officer said, looking at Cait with a blend of awe and respect. "The pervert won't be raping anyone else, that's for sure."

The idea was incomprehensible. Sloan stared down at her. "Cait?"

"I don't want to talk about it. Not now."

Dammit, she'd wanted to tell him in her own way. Seeing the shock on his face, Cait feared that having been forced to face the brutal, dark side of her work, Sloan might decide he couldn't love a woman capable of taking a life. Even in self-defense.

"Not now," he agreed.

He pressed his lips against a purple mark on her temple and struggled for calm. He wanted to curse. To rant. To rave. He wanted to go down to wherever they'd taken the creep's body and spit in his lifeless face.

With effort, Sloan reminded himself that she didn't need him to be going off like some crazed, half-cocked alpha male. What Cait needed now was tenderness. And love.

"Thanks for bringing her home," he told the officer.

"No problem." Realizing that three was definitely a crowd, the young patrolman backed out of the room, closing the door behind him.

"I was making dinner," Sloan said. Her hair was sandy and tangled with seaweed. He brushed it gently away from her battered face. "But it can wait. What would you say to a shower?"

She wrapped her arms around him and pressed her bruised cheek against his chest. "I'd say yes."

He turned on the shower and began to undress her slowly. Carefully. Easing the top over her head, sliding the pants down her legs. When he tossed the sandy sweats into the wastebasket, Cait opened her mouth to protest that they only needed washing, then realized she'd never be able to wear them again.

Stripping off his own clothes, he took her hand and drew her beneath the stream of warm water, adjusting the nozzle to a soft, gentle spray. Although the room and the water were warm, Cait was shivering.

She'd managed, just barely, to keep from screaming while waiting for the patrol cars to arrive after she'd called in the shooting. She'd also managed, somehow, to keep her composure during the inevitable questioning, although she'd been relieved when the commander of the special unit assured her that her report could wait until tomorrow.

The hardest thing had been not to shout at the young cop who'd rattled on during the drive to the apartment. Cait didn't feel much like a hero. Right now, she didn't even really feel much like a cop. Most of all, she just felt numb.

She stood there, trembling, as Sloan massaged the shampoo into her hair. "Poor baby," he murmured as the sand and seaweed disappeared down the drain.

He took her bar of French milled soap, rubbed it between his palms, and ran the perfumed bubbles over her body, stopping to press his lips against each piece of bruised flesh.

When his fingers brushed between her legs, she flinched.

"It's okay," he soothed, his hands as gentle as his voice. "You're okay."

Although she'd always sworn never to depend on any man, Cait found herself feeling so very grateful she'd had Sloan waiting at home for her.

"He didn't do anything," she said on a faint, fractured voice. "I mean, he didn't—" she drew in a painful breath "—rape me."

"Thank God." He was on his knees, spreading the lather down her legs like a silken veil. "For you." He surprised her by kissing her in the very same place where she'd flinched before. "But it wouldn't have mattered to me, Cait. Except for how it would have hurt you."

His lips had touched her this way before, and had always aroused her. This time, as she combed her fingers through his wet hair, she felt strangely soothed.

"Some men have trouble with the idea," she managed. "Of another man . . ." Her voice drifted off.

On some distant level Cait told herself that these tumultuous feelings she was experiencing would be helpful when she was assigned to the Sex Crimes Unit. But right now, it was difficult to think of anything except how close she'd come to being a victim herself. Never, in all her twenty-five years, had Cait ever felt as vulnerable as she had during that terrifying time beneath the pier.

Sloan lifted his head and looked up at her, his expression as sober, and as loving, as she'd ever seen it.

"I told you, sweet Cait," he said simply, "I love you."

It was then that she began to weep.

His heartfelt words opened emotional floodgates. Her hot tears continued to stream down her cheeks as he dried her off. As he carried her to bed.

"He killed the dog." The cocker spaniel's body had been found by a responding Malibu sheriff's deputy, floating at the water's edge. "He strangled it," she said, pushing the words past the painful lump in her throat. For some reason, she'd found that crime particularly horrifying. "It had served its purpose. And I suppose he was afraid it might try to protect me."

Not having the faintest idea what she was talking about, Sloan murmured soft soothing words meant to comfort as he continued to stroke her hair.

Finally, when she was all cried out, protected by the strong circle of Sloan's arms, Cait fell asleep.

The minute Blythe learned about the shooting from Natalie, who'd seen it on a televised newsbreak, she'd called the apartment, only to be told by Sloan the same thing Cait's mother had been told. Cait was sleeping.

When she offered to come by, he assured her that he had things well under control, that he expected an understandably emotionally exhausted Cait to be out like a light all night and suggested that Blythe call again in the morning.

As she hung up the phone, Blythe thought how strange it was to have Sloan taking charge that way. Strange, but nice, she decided. Independence was all very admirable and necessary, but she'd always thought Cait had a way of overdoing it.

Right now, if the news reports were even moderately accurate, she was grateful Cait had Sloan to take care of her.

Deciding that he was right, that there was no reason to cancel her plans, Blythe began to dress for Alan's long-awaited Hospital Board banquet.

Five hours later, she was standing in front of the window wall of her fiancé's Pacific Palisades home.

The living room had been professionally decorated in shades of gray, ranging from the muted silver of the walls to the deep pewter shade of the carpeting. Tasteful graphics—nothing too bold or avant garde—hung on the pale gray walls, illuminated by track lighting along the ten-foot ceiling.

The furniture, like the art, was contemporary. Italian black leather and molded, modular pieces covered in a muted black-and-gray striped upholstery blended perfectly with black lacquer bookshelves and glass-and-chrome tables that seemed to float atop the plush carpeting. A collection of small sculptures was displayed on glass-and-chrome shelves. The mood of the room was every bit as controlled as the man who lived there.

Moonlight created mysterious shadows in the mist that hung over the ocean. When she thought about how close Cait had come to dying down there, Blythe shivered.

"You're awfully quiet," a deep voice behind her offered.

She turned her head and smiled. "I'm sorry. I was thinking."

"About work," he guessed.

"No. Well, yes. In a way," she qualified. Knowing how he disapproved of Cait's work, she hadn't told him about today's dramatic events.

"You work too hard," he chided, handing her a balloon glass of clear liquor.

"You're probably right." Hawaii was sounding better and better. She could lie on the beach, soaking up rays, reading all the novels she'd been saving up, and drinking mai tais.

While she was away, Gage Remington could be digging up some cogent facts about Alexandra and Patrick. Then, when she returned to L.A., she'd be rested and ready to begin work on the star-crossed lovers' story.

Blythe sipped the brandy. "This is wonderful." She closed her eyes briefly, allowing the taste and bouquet to linger.

"One of my more grateful patients recently took a trip to France to celebrate her new face. She returned with a new husband—a French novelist twenty-five years her junior— and this fruit brandy from Alsace which she gave to me. I've been saving it for a special occasion."

She opened her eyes. "Oh, Alan, I'm sorry. I still haven't properly congratulated you on your award."

"Actually, you did," Alan allowed. "I seem to recall you slipping in it somewhere in that monologue about the private detective you hired."

She heard the trace of grievance in his voice and knew it was well deserved. "I really am sorry, darling," she said in her most conciliatory voice. "It's just that I was so excited that Gage has a lead on Alexandra's old makeup artist."

Realizing she was doing it again, Blythe clamped her teeth together. Hard. "But enough about me." She gave him her warmest smile. "Doctor of the Year is a very impressive award."

"True. But I'd give up the award in a moment in exchange for chief of surgery."

"You'll get it. After all, you're popular with the staff, you're definitely one of the most talented surgeons on staff—"

"One of?" he asked with a crooked smile.

"*The* most talented," she amended. "Why, when you began discussing your advances in brow lifts, you could have heard a pin drop for five tables around."

"That's lion country," he said proudly. "Working right over the brain. One slip of the scalpel and the patient's forehead is frozen like a zombie's."

"Well, I certainly wouldn't have the nerve to try it," Blythe said. "And everyone was very impressed to hear you're going to be featured in *Town and Country* as one of the top face makers in the country."

"It's nice PR," he allowed. "But I'm not certain it pulls much weight with Menninger."

Alan had always been deeply involved in hospital organization. He relished the politics involved, kept mental lists of who supported him and who opposed him and plotted his strategy with the precision of the Joint Chiefs of Staff preparing for armed invasion. She knew his ego was very much on the line in his current campaign to become chief of surgery.

"Dr. Menninger knows you're the best," she argued. "That's why he sent his wife to you. Speaking of which, she looks marvelous."

"She should. After all, the woman went from a size twelve to a size six," he said. "Martin's been complaining about the cost of all her new clothes but the way he's been dragging her to every social event of the season, I think he believes he's gotten his money's worth."

"He definitely has. And as for Sandra Longstreet," Blythe said, naming an Academy Award-winning actress in her late sixties, "she looked radiant. And fifteen years younger."

His chest puffed out at the compliment. "A deep plane procedure is a lot of work, but it's worth the extra time and effort. Before the lift, we had to break her jaw, move it down, with her teeth still attached, of course, and fix it in place with titanium plates and a graft of demineralized cow bone."

"That's amazing," Blythe said, honestly impressed even as she wondered what could possibly make a woman willing to suffer such pain solely in the name of vanity.

"I also transplanted fat from her thighs to around her mouth to fill in the wrinkles from all those years of smoking."

"You're definitely an artist, darling. The Michelangelo of the medical profession."

"Ah," he protested with a confident, practiced smile, "but Michelangelo could always throw away his mistakes."

They shared a laugh over that.

When he took the glass from her hand and placed it on the glass table in front of them, Blythe realized that the evening had just shifted from the professional to the personal.

"Did I mention that I love that dress?" he asked, running a long talented finger across her collarbone. The formal gown was a slender floor-length tube of gray silk, cut Grecian style, baring one pale shoulder.

"You should. Since you're the one who bought it."

"I wanted tonight to be perfect. Every doctor in the room was envious of me when I walked in with you on my arm." He made her sound like a second award he'd just won. Slightly depressed, Blythe slipped out of his light hold. "Is this new?" she asked, walking over to an ebony onyx figure of a nude set atop a black pedestal.

"I bought her last week," he allowed, his smooth controlled tone giving away neither the puzzlement nor the frustration she'd seen move across his eyes. "The minute I saw her in the gallery I realized that this is what I've always considered the perfect female form."

Blythe mentally compared the svelte female figure to her own curvaceous body. "You've no idea how that idea depresses me."

Alan laughed at that, a deep sound that was every bit as controlled as everything else about the man. "You've nothing to worry about, darling," he assured her. Crossing the room he took her in his arms. "Especially when you marry me."

"Are you saying that you'd want your wife fat and bare-foot in the kitchen?" she teased lightly.

"Gracious no!" He looked at her with mock horror. "I meant, that as the wife of a plastic surgeon, you could have all the nips and tucks you wanted."

Accustomed to control in his personal life, as well as his professional life, Alan closed the discussion by linking their fingers together and leading her into the bedroom. As in the rest of the luxurious apartment, glass and silver predominated, giving an almost operating-room sterility to the room.

Without preamble, he began to undress. First he placed the dinner jacket temporarily over a cedar stand. Blythe watched as those talented fingers dispensed with the ebony studs and matching cufflinks with the same deft skill he utilized in returning youthful beauty to a middle-aged society matron.

Instead of tossing the studs onto the nearest flat surface, as she would be apt to do, he placed them carefully away in the rosewood box atop a black lacquered chest.

Next came the bow tie, which joined the studs in the box. Then the shirt, which he folded before placing it in the woven hamper in the closet. The first time Blythe had seen him do this, she'd burst out laughing. When Alan had proven unamused, she'd learned to keep silent.

Still behaving as if he were all alone in the room, he sat down on the bed, took off his gleaming black dress shoes, which he slipped first into soft cloth protectors, then returned to their original box on the top shelf of the closet.

It was then that he looked up at her. "Is something wrong?"

She hadn't taken off so much as an earring. "No." It was a lie. Something was wrong. Blythe suddenly felt as if she were about to make love to a stranger. She forced a smile. "I thought it might be rather exciting to be undressed by the Doctor of the Year."

Her voice, made husky from uncharacteristic nervousness was one he'd never heard from her before. From the surprised, yet pleased expression that moved over his face, Blythe realized that he mistook her deepened tone for desire.

"Yes," he murmured thoughtfully, rubbing his chin as his eyes swept over her. "It might be a nice change, at that."

He rose from the bed and walked toward her, his stocking feet making no sound as they left long narrow footprints in the plush pewter carpeting.

He ran his fingers over her bare shoulder before dispensing with the back zipper with no less skill than she would have expected from one of *Town and Country*'s Top Ten facemakers. The dress slid down her body, a gray silk pool at her feet.

She stepped out of her high heels, allowing him to strip away her strapless silvery gray teddy trimmed with lace.

"Lord, you're sexy." He ran a palm up her leg, stroking the silky flesh above the lacy top of a thigh-high stocking. "If only all those old fossils in the surgery department could only see you now. You'd fill the CCU single-handedly."

Once again she felt uncomfortably like one of Alan's possessions. Once again Blythe tried to convince herself she was overreacting. It was just his way, she reminded herself.

"You don't need to give your opponents heart attacks to become chief of surgery."

He laughed at that. "Probably not. But perhaps we should keep it in mind. As a last resort."

Dispatching with the rest of his own clothes, he drew her down onto the gray-and-white pinstriped sheets and lay down beside her.

Blythe waited for the expected warmth and was disappointed. It would come, she assured herself. The trick was to relax.

The only sound in the room was the occasional rustle of Egyptian cotton sheets, and their breathing—his rough and ragged, hers distressingly even. Try as she might to lose herself in the moment, and the man, arousal proved illusive.

He looked down at her, his gaze puzzled and shadowed with disappointment. "Tell me what you want."

"You." She wrapped her arms around his neck and pressed her open mouth against his. Wantonly, desperately, her legs captured him in a vicelike grip. "I want you."

His hands slid beneath her hips and he thrust into her, claiming possession of her body, even as her rebellious mind remained out of reach.

Blythe arched against him and called out his name on a fractured, broken sound.

She was, after all, a superb actress.

When he felt her body shudder, Alan gave in to his own release, collapsing onto her with a groan of satisfaction.

"Alan?" Blythe whispered some time later. Although she hated to complain, he was getting heavy.

His only response was a soft snore, making her realize he'd fallen asleep.

Blythe had planned to spend the night. But after she'd lain awake for hours, listening to her fiance's deep breathing and the sound of the surf below the steep cliff, she left the bed and gathered up her discarded clothing.

She left him a brief note. Then drove home. Alone.

IT WAS SNOWING *in Telluride, Colorado. Fat, white flakes floated down from the night sky like feathers. Overhead, a full moon cast a shimmering silver glow over the frosty landscape.*

The only sounds were the crunch of sleigh runners across the snowy ground, the huff of the horse's breath and the jingle of harness bells.

Beneath the thick lap rug, Alexandra snuggled up against her new husband and wondered what she'd ever done to have fate bless her so.

"I'm so happy." She smiled up at him. Her face, surrounded by the lush white ermine hood, was glowing with all the heartfelt emotion she was feeling. Her smile was nothing less than beatific; snowflakes glistened like diamonds in her thick dark eyelashes.

Patrick smiled down at her. "I was worried you'd regret not having an elaborate Hollywood wedding."

The idea of eloping to Arizona had proven ideal. After the brief ceremony, wanting to postpone the press blitzkrieg they both knew they'd face, they'd driven her Rolls to Colorado.

Now, five days into an idyllic honeymoon, Alexandra knew they'd made the right decision. Their love was too special to share with others.

"My only regret is that we have to go back at all," she said. The truth of her words was echoed in her liquid dark eyes.

"We don't have to." His expression was absolutely serious. "Not if you'd really rather not." Patrick's willingness to turn his back on fame and fortune was one of the reasons she'd fallen in love with him. She'd never met a man who loved her just for herself, instead of her looks, or her perceived sexuality, or what she could do to boost his career.

"I know you mean that." Alexandra also realized that if he did back out of the deal with Xanadu Studios, Walter Stern would make Patrick pay in ways she couldn't begin to imagine. The man was ruthless. She had not a single doubt that if she ever crossed him, he would step on her with no more thought than he would a cockroach.

It was going to be bad enough when he learned about the elopement. By following her heart, she'd already risked Patrick paying for her own act of rebellion. She certainly wasn't about to make things worse by costing Xanadu its biggest project of the year.

Forcing an encouraging smile, she pressed her gloved palm against his cheek. "You've written a wonderful book, Patrick. And it's going to make a marvelous movie."

"With you as the star, how can it miss?"

"We make a good team."

"The best." He put his arm around her and drew her closer. "I suppose you're right about seeing the film through," he agreed reluctantly. "I did give my word."

Unlike so many other men she'd known, Alexandra understood that to Patrick, his word was a sacred bond. Knowing how he felt had made their wedding vows even more special.

"But after it's wrapped, I'm insisting on taking you away for a real honeymoon," he promised. "How would you like to take a Grand Tour to Europe?"

Knowing also how her rugged American cowboy felt about any artifice, she couldn't envision him happily sipping champagne cocktails at some Paris sidewalk cafe. But he would, she knew. For her.

"Do you want the truth?"

"Absolutely."

"I'd rather go to your ranch." Linking her hands around his neck, she kissed him. "I want you to show me Wyoming."

Her tongue circled his mouth. Their breath, rising like little white ghosts on the icy night air, mingled.

"I want to learn to fish for trout, with those pretty make-believe flies you're always tying and I want to take long hikes with you in the mountains and I want to ride horses."

He slipped his hand beneath the blanket. "How about riding your husband?" he asked huskily.

As he pressed his hand against that secret place, heat flared, making her forget all about the cold.

Her answering laugh was filled with sensual promise. "Absolutely."

Surrendering to the power of her husband's exquisite kisses, Alexandra closed her eyes and imagined she heard bells ringing.

And ringing. And ringing. The chimes of the telephone filtered into her consciousness, jerking Blythe from a deep sleep.

"Hello?" The sheets were hopelessly tangled and she had her arms wrapped around her pillow as if it were her lover. Her mind was still fogged with the sensuality of her dream. "Oh, good morning, Gage.

"No," she lied, struggling to a sitting position. The pillow slid off onto the floor. "Of course you didn't wake me. I've been up for hours."

She dragged her hand through her tangled hair and tried to concentrate on what he was saying, which was difficult when his husky voice was strumming sensual chords she told herself were left over from her dream.

"You've found her? Really? Where?"

When Blythe heard where the former makeup artist was living, she was stunned. "Bachelor Arms? That's Cait's building."

She shook her head in disbelief as she thought about how many times she'd visited Bachelor Arms in the past weeks. To find out that Natasha Kuryan was the elderly, eccentric woman Cait had mentioned that first day was incredible.

"Of course I want to meet with her." She glanced over at the clock. "Why don't I meet you there in an hour?"

Blythe hung up. But the brief conversation stayed with her all during her shower and while she dressed.

It was only as she drove to Bachelor Arms that Blythe realized that Gage Remington's voice bore a remarkable resemblance to Patrick Reardon's in her dream.

12

THE SUN WAS STREAMING through the window when Cait finally woke. She opened her eyes, her gaze colliding with Sloan's. He'd obviously been up for some time. Long enough to shower and shave and dress.

"Hi." She felt suddenly, strangely, shy.

"Hi." He eyed her with concern. "How are you feeling?"

"Okay, I guess." She looked at the bedside clock, groaned, and hitched herself up in bed. "I'm late. I was due at headquarters an hour ago."

"I already called and told them you'd be in later." Her hair had dried into a mass of ungovernable red waves.

"What did they say?"

"After the day you had yesterday, what could they say?" He brushed the tousled curls away from her face with a heartbreakingly tender touch. "How are you feeling?"

"Fine." At his disbelieving look, she said, "All right, I'm a little sore. But I'm okay."

He was more concerned about her mental health. Although she'd been trained to blow bad guys away, Sloan didn't believe Cait could easily shrug off killing another human being.

He pulled her closer, fitting her against him. "Your captain left a number for you to call later."

"The police shrink," she guessed flatly.

"It probably wouldn't hurt to talk about it."

"Talking won't change anything."

"No. But it might help with the nightmares."

Her eyes widened. A vague memory stirred, but she'd been so out of it . . . "Did I—"

"You had three, that I could count," he informed her. "None of them very pleasant. Just think about it, okay?" Sloan traced her downturned lips with a fingertip.

"All right."

She snuggled against him, savoring his warmth. His strength. They remained quiet for a long, pleasurable time. Once again Cait considered how fortunate she was to have this man in her life.

"Thank you." It was barely a whisper.

"For what?"

"For loving me."

He pressed his lips against her tousled hair. "Hell, that's the easy part."

While she'd been sleeping so restlessly, he'd lain awake, thinking of all she'd been through, thinking of how he was going to tell her the dark, hidden secrets she deserved to know. Ugly truths that might drive her away.

"There's someone I want you to meet," he said later, as Cait dressed, getting ready to go downtown.

"Sure."

Having never seen her dressed for work in anything but undercover clothes, Sloan was relieved when the sight of the dark blue uniform didn't cause an instantaneous, knee-jerk response. How much had changed in less than three short weeks, he mused. How much he had changed.

"I thought maybe this evening," he suggested. "If you feel up to it, after your debriefing."

The strangely guarded tone made Cait stop in the act of tying her black shoes to glance up at him. His expression could have been cut from granite. But there was a vulnerability in his eyes that tugged at some elemental chord deep inside her.

"Sloan? What's wrong?"

Although she'd assured him—and the captain had confirmed during their phone conversation—that the debriefing was merely routine, Sloan knew that having to relive such a horrifying incident was bound to be incredibly difficult.

Feeling like a world-class jerk for giving her one more thing to worry about while she was on her way to headquarters to answer questions about yesterday's officer-involved shooting, he forced a smile. "Nothing." He crossed to where she was sitting on the edge of the bed, bent down and kissed her. Desire stirred. He tamped it down.

"How about letting me drive you to headquarters?"

Cait opened her mouth to assure him it wasn't necessary. Then, as last night's terror came flooding back, she changed her mind. "I'd love to have you with me. But I may be a long time."

"I'll wait." He brushed his lips against hers in a soft, reassuring way. "For as long as it takes."

They both knew he wasn't talking about her meeting with police brass.

"I CAN'T BELIEVE THIS!" Blythe stormed as she marched away from Bachelor Arms. Her frustration surrounded her like a crackling electrical field. Beside her, Gage reluctantly decided that although he'd never believed it possible, right now the actress was actually sexier than she appeared up on that larger-than-life silver screen. As she raked her hand furiously through her dark hair, he caught the glimpse of a very good quality four-carat diamond engagement ring. *She's also taken, pal,* he reminded himself. And even if she wasn't, Blythe Fielding was definitely out of his league.

"Hey, it's only a little setback." Ten years in the police department, and another six months running his own detective agency, had taught Gage patience.

"The clock is ticking, dammit. I only have seven more months to get this project to the editing stage. Then I'm scheduled to do another picture for Walter Stern." Her frustration etched deep lines into her forehead. "We don't have time for any setbacks." When he didn't answer, Blythe shook her head in disgust. "What kind of old lady takes a cruise to Greece?"

"I think cruising is pretty popular with the senior crowd," Gage suggested mildly.

Irritated that Gage was taking this so well, Blythe glared up at him. "I'm sure the fact that you're being paid by the day has nothing to do with your willingness to let this investigation drag on forever," she ground out.

The fact that he'd taken a lot worse verbal abuse on L.A.'s mean streets kept Gage from being overly angered by her insinuation that he'd cheat her. Early training supported by years of experience had taught him that escalating the antagonism level did nothing to diffuse a difficult situation. Instead, he gave her a steady, bland look.

"If I thought you meant that, I'd suggest you take your movie—and your enigmatic Russian movie star—to some other P.I."

His tone was annoyingly calm. As was his expression. But looking up at him, Blythe could sense the flintiness of his gaze behind the sunglasses. She also heard the edge of steel in those mild words.

Her shoulders slumped. "I'm sorry. It's just that I was so excited when you called and told me you'd found her." She glared back at the pink apartment building. "Why couldn't Natasha Kuryan be the kind of old lady who spends her days in print cotton housedresses crocheting scratchy afghans?"

"Now you're talking about my great-grandmother," he said. "Who's still happily living in the same house where she was born ninety-seven years ago in Show Low, Arizona and never misses Wednesday night choir practice or Saturday night bingo."

He gave her a slow, friendly grin. "And as much as I love Gram to pieces, she never, in a million years, would have considered moving to Hollywood and trying to get a job putting makeup on movie stars."

His smile captured Blythe's attention, reminding her suddenly of this morning's sensual dream. She felt the warm color rising beneath her cheeks and hoped Gage would take it for lingering anger.

"Point taken," she said. "So, now what?"

"The super said she'll be back in five days."

"In five days I'll be in Maui."

On her honeymoon. It crossed Gage's mind that she didn't exactly sound real eager about the prospect. Reminding himself that Blythe's relationship with her fiancé was none of his business, he shrugged.

"Don't worry about it. I'll talk to her, then fill you in on all the details when you get back."

"If Natasha knew Alexandra, I don't want to wait until I return. I want to know everything you find out right away."

"Fine. I'll fax you at the hotel."

"I'd rather you call."

Gage considered how less than thrilled he'd be if his new bride was spending their honeymoon talking on the telephone with another man and decided that the good Dr. Sturgess must possess a great deal of patience.

"Fine. It's your nickel. If you want to pay for long distance calls, it's okay by me." He glanced down at his watch. "In the meantime, how about lunch? I've run across some discrepancies in the bio Xanadu concocted for Alexandra.

Which wouldn't have been unusual for the time," he allowed, telling Blythe nothing she didn't already know. "It opens up a few leads I'm thinking of pursuing. But I need your okay first."

"You're the detective," she pointed out. "Do what you have to do."

"It could be expensive. I'll have to fly to Florida."

He'd piqued her interest. Blythe consulted her own watch, thought of her appointment with the florist in thirty minutes, then made her decision.

"How about Le Chardonnay?" she suggested. The art deco Restaurant on Melrose Avenue was an unabashed copy of a Left Bank bistro, circa 1920. The booths were cozy and comfortable, reminding Blythe of the kind of Provençal atmosphere Alexandra might have favored. "I suddenly have a craving for their roast duckling Mirabelle."

Despite a high noise level, Gage knew the restaurant to be a perfect spot for romantic afternoon rendezvous. Reminding himself that this lunch date was strictly business, he said, "I've always believed in satisfying cravings."

CAIT'S DEBRIEFING proved to be as routine as promised. Her automatic suspension was immediately rescinded, although the captain did suggest she take a few days of personal leave, an offer she accepted. Perhaps, she considered, after Blythe's wedding, she and Sloan could spend the weekend at her mother's beach cottage in Avalon, on Catalina Island.

There were times, Cait admitted, when it was rather nice to have rich parents. She certainly couldn't have afforded the remote getaway on a patrolman's salary.

Not that she was going to be a patrolman for long. To her amazement, she'd been informed that her superior was recommending a battlefield promotion to detective. Along with her promised transfer to the Sex Crimes Unit.

"I've never made love to a detective before," Sloan murmured, as they drove up the Pacific Coast Highway. The sanitarium was in Malibu, just north of Pepperdine University.

They'd stopped by the apartment after the debriefing, only long enough for Cait to change into a colorful silk tunic and knife-pleated skirt that reminded Sloan of a brilliant summer sunset.

"Play your cards right, and you may get lucky tonight," Cait advised. The gleam in her eyes seconded the sensual promise.

Sloan reached out between them, took her hand in his and hoped that she'd still be in his life tonight.

There was something definitely wrong with Sloan. The tension simmering beneath the surface Cait had felt this morning had escalated to a barely restrained anxiety that made every nerve in her body feel as if it were standing on end.

The uncomfortable silence hovered over them, like a storm threatening on the horizon until Cait felt ready to scream. She was tempted to beg him to at least give her some clue as to where they were going, and why, but managed to hold her tongue. It was obvious that Sloan intended to tell his story his own way. In his own time.

She recognized the white gates immediately, having visited various friends—and a stepmother and various stepsiblings—at the facility over the years. The sanitarium's substance abuse program was second only in popularity among the movie crowd to Camp Betty.

She watched as Sloan was greeted by the guard at the gate like an old friend. Similar greetings were also offered by both staff and patients as they made their way across the emerald green lawn.

Sloan stopped suddenly, took her hand and turned her toward him. Although his expression remained unreadable, his icy hand betrayed his uncharacteristic nervousness.

"Will you do me one favor?"

"Anything." It was the truth.

"Whatever happens, will you not mention you're a police officer?"

"Of course," she said promptly, still puzzled. "If that's what you want."

He dragged his free hand down his face. "It's not what I'd prefer. But sometimes we don't get what we want."

With that inexplicable statement, he started walking again. Cait saw they were headed toward a woman seated on a bench, looking out at the sunset-gilded sea.

When she turned toward them, Cait realized that she was beautiful. Her complexion, tinged to a pale golden hue from the sun, was nearly flawless, her jaw still firm. Her honey blond hair had been cut in a sleek, chin-length bob that swung gracefully when she turned her head. As she took off her sunglasses, Cait also realized where Sloan had gotten his whiskey-colored eyes.

A realization that was confirmed when Sloan bent down, kissed the woman's cheek, then said, "Mom, I'd like you to meet Caitlin Carrigan. The woman I love." He turned to Cait. "Cait, this is my mother. Laura Wyndham Riley."

The name rang an instantaneous bell. As Cait wondered how in the world Sloan had managed to keep such a secret in a town that thrived on gossip, the woman held out her hand with a gracious dignity that bespoke her patrician roots.

"Hello, Caitlin. It's a pleasure to meet you." Her smile was soft and charming. It also did not quite reach her vague brown eyes. She turned to Sloan. "Your father will be so happy to know you've found someone to love." She turned back to Cait. "He's always wanted to be a grandfather," she confided.

Cait smiled even as her eyes misted. For this poor, damaged woman. But more for Sloan. "So has my father," she lied deftly.

As she looked at him, Sloan knew that he would never love her more than he did at that moment.

For the next hour, Laura chattered gaily about her youthful days as Philadelphia's most sought-after debutante, about the way she'd fallen in love with Sloan's father. About the happiness they shared.

And even as Cait smiled and nodded and smiled some more, she felt as if her heart were breaking.

"How long has she been that way?" she asked quietly, as they walked back to his Porsche after the nurse had taken Laura in to dinner.

"Actually, you're seeing her on one of her good days. There are times she can't talk at all. Times I don't even know if she hears me." He sighed as he opened the passenger door. "And she's been that way since my father died."

"But that's been . . ." Her voice trailed off as she attempted to remember.

"Fifteen years."

She did some quick mental arithmetic. "When you were sixteen." Formative years for a young boy and a tender time to lose his father, Cait considered. But to lose him in such a brutal, public way . . .

"We woke up one morning to find the house surrounded by federal agents and Portland cops." Sloan was looking out over the cliff, but she suspected it was not the Pacific Ocean he was seeing. "Mom begged Dad to turn himself in, to just finally end things, so we could have some semblance of a normal life, but he'd thought of himself as a renegade for too long. Kind of like Billy the Kid, still fighting the establishment."

The story of Buck Riley's violent death, after years of hiding in the anti-Vietnam war underground, was the stuff legends—and movies—were made of. In fact, Cait realized, a movie had been made about his father's illegal activities. That same documentary had catapulted Sloan to stardom.

"That's why your *Arlington Seven* was so emotionally riveting," she said when he'd joined her in the close confines of the sports car. The story of the man who'd robbed banks, plotted to bomb the Pentagon and driven the getaway car during a holdup that had resulted in a bank guard being killed, had been about Sloan's father.

Just as the subplot about the debutante who'd turned her back on wealth and privilege for a life on the run with an ex-convict had obviously been written about that lovely, fragile woman she'd just met. "Because you wrote it from firsthand experience."

"My father's trial was before I was born." Sloan sighed. "I was conceived while he was in custody."

Cait, more than most people, knew the idea was not as impossible as it sounded. "A guard sneaked your mother into the jail," she guessed.

"For a hefty price." His smile was grim, suggesting that sometimes it was difficult to tell the supposed good guys from the bad guys. "I was born after his escape."

She shook her head as she took the amazing thought in. "You must have spent your life on the run."

"Most of it," he concurred. "Until the entire thing blew up in our faces. I ended up in foster care, but I ran away the first year. Mom was put in a state mental hospital in Salem, Oregon. As soon as I started making money, I bailed her out and brought her here."

Cait, who'd always bemoaned her own unstable life, couldn't begin to imagine what Sloan's must have been like. "What about her parents? Why didn't they take you in? Why didn't they pay her hospital bills?"

His expression was grim. "The Wyndhams disowned Mom when she took up with my father. Nothing that happened afterward changed their minds."

Although Cait knew her mother deplored her chosen career, she also knew, deep down, that Natalie was proud of her. She also knew that there was nothing she could ever do—including turning urban terrorist and robbing banks—that could make her mother stop loving her. "How did you go to school?"

"Sometimes Mom taught me at home. Other times, if the administration wasn't too picky about records, I'd get to attend regular classes for a while. By the time I was in the fifth grade, I'd been to twelve different grammar schools under twelve different names."

She thought about all Sloan had missed, thought about how such an existence would have precluded having friends, thought about moving from place to place, always one step ahead of the law. . . .

"Oh, my God," she groaned. "I just realized what you meant about the irony of me being a cop."

He managed a crooked smile and ran his palm down her hair. "I was brought up to have a fairly unflattering view of your profession."

"I'm not surprised." She remembered all too vividly the newsreel footage Sloan had spliced into his documentary, recalled the sight of Buck Riley's body on his front lawn, riddled with bullets.

"I'm amazed that you didn't turn out to be some kind of cold-blooded, antisocial murderer," she murmured.

"You know what they say." He shrugged. "What doesn't kill you makes you strong." He glanced back the way they'd come. "I just wish. . . ." His voice drifted off and he dragged his hands through his hair. "Hell."

"Your mother, in her own way, is a very lucky woman," Cait said softly. "I doubt many women have sons who love them so unconditionally."

She felt her eyes filling with hot moisture again.

Sloan watched the tear trailing down her cheek and brushed it away with the pad of his thumb. "I was worried you might not want to be with me anymore. When you learned who I really was."

"I know who you are." She caught his hand in hers and pressed her lips against his palm, her eyes earnest as they met his in the slanting glow of the setting sun. "The man I love."

He closed his eyes and breathed a soft sigh of relief. "You are incredible."

"Not half as incredible as you," she said and meant it.

"Well." He took another deep breath and seemed to shake off the sadness that had settled over them. "You'll obviously have more questions, but I promised you dinner. You name it, sweetheart. Tonight the sky's the limit."

Cait didn't want to go out to some trendy Hollywood hot spot. She didn't want to share Sloan with anyone. What she wanted was so show him exactly how much she loved him.

"How hungry are you?" she asked.

He shrugged. "Not terribly. Why?"

"Because I'd rather go home. And send out for Chinese later." She leaned across the console separating them and pressed her lips against his. "Much, much later."

When the long heartfelt kiss finally ended, Sloan twisted the key in the ignition. "I love Chinese."

The minute they entered her bedroom, Cait turned and gave him a slow, wet kiss.

She desperately needed to make love to Sloan, to prove to him how very much she loved him. More than ever, after the intimate secret he'd shared with her. Also, after yesterday's traumatic experience, she needed to prove to herself that she was truly alive and safe.

Her hands trembled as she unbuttoned his shirt, slipping it off his shoulders and down his arms, forgetting at first to unfasten the cuff buttons. Having undressed more than a few women in his life, Sloan knew the awkwardness of wrestling with unfamiliar fasteners and felt it immensely touching that Cait was so willing to do so now. The shirt finally fluttered to the floor, like a snowy bird.

When her palms skimmed down his torso, Sloan closed his eyes and sucked in his stomach, waiting for her to move on to his jeans. But she surprised him by kneeling on the flowered needlepoint rug to attack the laces of his running shoes.

After dispensing with his shoes and socks, she slowed the pace again, running her hands over his chest, his shoulders, his back. Sloan wondered why he'd ever believed that men should take off their own clothing. Why he'd believed that shedding clothes faster made things better. More efficient.

The care Cait was taking in undressing him made him feel immensely special. Like a package worth savoring. And even as he told himself that after all she'd suffered last night, he should be the one pleasuring her, not the other way around, he found himself surrendering to her sweet torment.

Finally, when his heart was beginning to pound and his skin had grown moist, she managed, with increasing skill, to finesse the jeans over his hips. Then his white cotton briefs.

Naked and needy, he reached for her, but she seemed determined to maintain the ritual. Backing away, just out of reach, she began shedding her own clothes with a slowly seductive air the head stripper at Paris's Folies Bergère would have envied.

He watched, entranced, as she pulled her silk tunic over her head, revealing a flower-sprigged demi-bra trimmed in ivory lace that was worlds different from the white cotton underwear she'd worn to Maine. Through the sheer fabric he could see her taut, rosy nipples and the darker aureoles surrounding them.

"I think this is where I tell you that I really, really like that," he managed.

She answered his with a sultry smile. "It's just a little something I bought the day Blythe and I went shopping." Her eyes on his, the smile still on her full lips, she leaned forward slightly, reaching behind her back to unfasten the skimpy bra.

She held it against her chest with one hand for a long, suspended moment. Then she let it fall to the floor where it landed atop his shirt, revealing breasts he was literally dying to touch. To taste.

With another siren's smile, she stepped out of her shoes. Her skirt was next. Sloan decided that the whisper of silk being whisked over bare skin was the sexiest sound he'd ever heard.

She was standing in front of him, clad only in a pair of skimpy flowered panties that made her legs look as if they went on forever.

Leaving them on for now, she took his hand, drawing him down to the bed, where she continued her tender torment.

Her lips plucked at a hard brown nipple and Sloan groaned. Her tongue took a long wet swathe at the inside of his thighs, causing an oath to explode from him.

Having come to know his body well during these past nights, Cait touched Sloan where it would give the most pleasure. Tasted in a slow, seductive way that turned that pleasure to grinding ache.

She slid sleekly, agilely down his body and as her hands and mouth moved over him, Sloan forgot control, surrendered his power. His pulse thundered beneath her lips. With every ragged breath he took, her scent slammed into him.

The desire was as strong as always. But less urgent. Sloan had never known need could be so unbearably sweet. Or passion so exquisitely patient. Never had he been so aware of his body as he was now, as Cait explored it so slowly. So thoroughly.

He belonged to her, Sloan realized as emotions coursed through him, every bit as much as he'd wanted her to belong to him.

The softness of her mouth against his heated flesh was like a soft summer breeze. After she'd drawn out all his secrets, after she'd stripped him of all his defenses, Cait took his penis in her hands.

Entranced, she traced the dark purple vein with first her fingernail, and then her tongue. She felt power in the knowledge that she could create such hunger. Freedom in knowing that she could take as much as she wanted, could do whatever she wished, and he'd still want her. Still love her.

"Look," he managed to say on a ragged groan.

Cait followed his gaze to the gilded mirror standing in the corner across the room and realized that the image was, at the same time, both the most exciting and beautiful thing she'd ever seen. Cait knew that the sight would stay with her for the rest of her life.

Sloan was no less affected. The sight of her rosy wet lips embracing him in the most intimate kiss of all was almost more than he could bear. Gripping her hips, he tore her panties away, then drew her up so her knees were braced on either side of his thighs. As he looked at her in the mirror, poised above him, her flesh damp and glowing, her eyes gleaming with passion, her hair a glorious gleaming tangle, Sloan knew he'd remember Cait this way. Always.

He lowered her down slowly, filling her inch by devastating inch. A perfect fit, they merged, male to female, their united rhythm ancient and beautiful.

13

TWO DAYS BEFORE Blythe's wedding, she and Cait drove to the airport to meet Lily's plane.

It had been three years since either of them had seen their college friend. "Do you realize," Cait said as they watched the passengers stream from the jetway, "that the last time we were all together was for Lily's wedding?"

"It seems like yesterday," Blythe murmured, remembering the fateful day all too well.

Lily, dressed in a billowy cloud of hand-beaded silk organza that had undoubtedly cost more than the Padgett family farm back in Iowa, had looked as if she'd stepped from the gilded pages of a fairy tale.

"I'll bet to Lily it's seemed an eternity," Cait muttered, glaring at one blue-suited passenger who'd slowed to take a longer, second interested look at her.

"I wonder why she never said anything," Blythe mused. Lily had looked so happy that day, Blythe considered sadly. So blissfully in love. "About her marriage being unhappy."

Cait shrugged. "Beats me. She was always the most outgoing of the three of us." Lily Padgett's warm, generous heart and open, gregarious midwestern ways had contributed to her immense charm. Apparently it had also contributed to her downfall, Cait mused.

There had been a time, only a few weeks ago, when she would have used Lily's tragic mistake as additional proof that giving away your heart could only result in pain. But now those days seemed a lifetime ago. Before Sloan.

"It's sad thinking of her keeping such a dark secret."

"We should have been there," Blythe stated firmly.

"I should have shot him," Cait said, just as firmly.

They had no more time to discuss it as Lily finally appeared. It crossed Blythe's mind that she should have exited the plane sooner, with the other first class passengers, but then the three women were hugging and kissing and crying and the thought was immediately forgotten.

After collecting Lily's luggage, Blythe drove them to Venice, where they ate grilled chicken and roasted red pepper pizza at the Sidewalk café on the ocean front. Although there were certainly more glamorous spots to dine in Los Angeles, Blythe had thought her friend might get a kick out of the small restaurant that had long been a hangout for L.A.'s most eclectic creative community.

"This is wonderful," Lily said with a long, drawn out sigh as she settled down at an open-air table.

"You must be exhausted." Blythe's judicious gaze swept over Lily's pale features. She was still lovely, with her long hair fashioned in a French braid that fell nearly to her waist and her wide blue eyes. But before her marriage, she'd been bright and lively, a literal whirlwind of activity that belied her fragility of looks. Now, in contrast, she seemed merely fragile.

"It was a long flight," Lily agreed with a faint smile that was worlds different from the bright and sunny one Blythe and Cait were used to seeing. "And the baby seemed determined to jog all the way from Kennedy to LAX." She pressed her palms against her swollen belly.

"I still can't believe that you're pregnant," Blythe said, wanting more than anything to touch Lily's rounded stomach, but unwilling to invade her space without being invited. "It must be the most amazing feeling." Remembering all Lily had been through in these past months, Blythe guiltily tapped down the faint envy that stirred through her.

This time Lily's smile reached her weary eyes. "Amazing. And exhausting."

Blythe had been right when she'd given her opinion that Lily was upset about something, Cait determined. Something was very wrong.

"So, are you going to tell us what the problem is?" she asked with her typical forthrightness. "Or are we going to spend the rest of the day playing twenty questions?"

"I don't know what you're talking about," Lily hedged, proving herself a miserable liar. She turned her attention to the row of psychics who'd set up shop at card tables along the sidewalk. "I've always wanted to have my fortune told."

"My treat," Cait said. "After you tell us what's got you so depressed. Besides the obvious, of course."

"Nothing." Her unpainted lip began to tremble. "Really. It's just that it was a long flight, and I'm still trying to get over Junior's death, and—"

"Junior was a womanizer," Cait argued. "For Pete's sake, Lily, the man was with his mistress when his car ran off that bridge."

Lily lifted her chin but her eyes watered. "He was my husband."

It was bad enough that she was on the verge of crying. Again! Lily absolutely refused to put a pall over Blythe's wedding by revealing how much she hated her dead husband for leaving her—and their child—at the mercy of his icy but horrendously treacherous parents. Once again her hands settled on her stomach, this time the gesture one of maternal protection.

"Stop subjecting Lily to the third degree," Blythe instructed Cait firmly. "She's flown all the way across the country and she's undoubtedly worn-out." She reached out and patted Lily's hand, which was no longer adorned by the diamond solitaire Junior had given her for an engagement ring.

Although Blythe now knew, without a shadow of a doubt, that something was terribly wrong, she didn't want to push. "Meanwhile," she said, "let me fill you in on the plans for the wedding. Such as they are."

Blythe was grateful when Lily did not point out the obvious lack of planning given to the ceremony. She could only hope that her friend assumed that all California weddings were taken more casually than her own New York one had been.

Although Lily had professed a desire to get married in Iowa, in the Methodist church where she'd attended Sunday school, where her parents had sung in the choir every Sunday morning, she'd been quickly and firmly overruled by her future in-laws. They had pointed out that a rural wedding would make it impossible for their numerous friends and business acquaintances to attend.

Desperately in love, and seemingly born with a desire to please, Lily had caved in without putting forth any argument. It was better this way, she'd assured Cait and Blythe, who'd both counseled her to have the wedding she wanted. There was no way her farmer parents could afford even a small wedding, let alone the elaborate ceremony the Van Cortlandts were expecting.

Which was why, on a rainy summer morning, Lily and J. Carter Van Cortlandt, had exchanged vows to a packed crowd in the Gothic Revival-style St. Thomas Episcopal Church on Fifth Avenue.

Lily looked up from the single page of typed paper. "Do you love Alan, Blythe?" she asked suddenly.

"Of course." Blythe ignored Cait's grimace. "I wouldn't be marrying him if I didn't love him."

"And does he love you?"

"Of course."

"Does he make you crazy?"

"If you mean does he have any nagging little flaws—"

"No." Lily leaned forward, her gaze turning inordinately serious. "I mean, in bed. Does he drive you mad when you make love?"

Remembering all too well that Lily, ignoring all the young men who'd tried to change her mind, had insisted on going to her nuptial bed a virgin, such a question surprised Blythe.

"That's a rather personal question, Lily," she said softly, glancing around to see if anyone else had heard them.

"You and Cait always told me about the men you slept with," Lily pressed on, seemingly determined to discover the truth. "Why should this be any different?"

"Because Alan's different." Just as she'd hedged when Cait had asked a similar question, Blythe was not about to admit to those times when she'd felt vaguely disappointed after their lovemaking. "He's the man I love, Lily. The man I'm gong to spend the rest of my life with. I don't feel comfortable sharing our intimate moments. Not even with you."

Lily gave her another long, unfathomable look. "I suppose I can understand that," she decided finally. "And I realize I don't have all that much experience, but the one thing I have learned, Blythe, is that if a man can't make you fly, and you can't make him burn, you're probably letting yourself in for a lot of pain down the road."

Cait realized that with that single statement, Lily had told them more about her marriage than she'd intended. She also made Cait realize exactly how special her lovemaking with Sloan was. Although Lily was right about Blythe and Cait having experienced more lovers, never had Cait ever met a man who could make her fly like Sloan Wyndham.

That thought led to another. Sloan's belief, which was admittedly seeming less crazy by the day, that they were destined to spend their lives together.

For the next hour, the trio gossiped about old schoolmates over lunch, watched the parade of in-line skaters and joggers as they indulged in gooey hot fudge sundaes, after which they had their fortunes told by three separate psychics, each of whom assured them that after a few heartbreaks, they would all find true love, wealth and fame.

"The hell with the love and fame," Lily decided as they walked back to the beachfront lot where Blythe had parked her car. "I'll take the wealth." Her tone was, for her, strangely firm.

Cait and Blythe exchanged a brief look, both remembering the young farm girl who'd never professed any desire for money. Which had made the fact that she'd married into one of the wealthiest families on the eastern seaboard even more surprising.

Once again Blythe reminded herself this was not the time to delve into the obvious changes in Lily.

"I'll settle for fame," she decided, already secretly imagining Alexandra Romanov's story rocketing her into the lofty realm of Academy Award-winning producers.

"I guess that leaves me with love," Cait decided.

Knowing Cait's feelings on the subject, Lily and Blythe both laughed. Wondering what they'd say if they knew she actually considered it the best choice of the three, Cait merely grinned.

For that suspended, perfect moment, they could have been back in college, sharing a giggle while studying for finals.

Unfortunately, Lily thought sadly, as Blythe drove up into the hills after the lengthy, enjoyable lunch, life didn't stop when things seemed perfect. Like the age-old rhythm of the sea, it continued its eternal ebb and flow.

Whether you wanted it to or not.

THE DAY FOR THE WEDDING dawned bright and clear and sunny. Although Alan had wanted a large church wedding to which he'd be able to invite numerous members of the hospital staff, in the end, he'd settled—begrudgingly—for a private affair with close friends in Blythe's garden.

Once again it was like old times as the three women dressed and primped for the ceremony together in Blythe's second-floor bedroom.

Outside, a harpist, hired for the occasion, was entertaining the small gathering of family and guests seated on the rented satin-covered chairs. Beneath a white arbor emblazoned with scarlet Don Juan roses, Alan stood tall and straight, with his groomsman—another doctor—by his side, waiting for his bride to join him.

He looked extremely handsome in his dark suit, Blythe considered, looking down at him from behind the French doors leading out to the balcony. His blond hair gleamed golden in the sun, the random strands of silver glistened attractively.

I love him, Blythe told herself. *I do. Truly.* Oh, he could be a bit stuffy from time to time, she admitted. But she'd much rather her husband be accused of being dull than carousing around like some out-of-control adolescent.

As for the fact that Alan didn't really appreciate her work, Blythe knew she could be accused of possessing tunnel vision from time to time. Especially like now, when she was working on a project she cared deeply about. Without Alan around to complain, she could easily become one of those grim, humorless, driven females Joan Crawford used to portray in those black-and-white career woman movies.

Alan was good for her, Blythe assured herself yet again. He'd be a decent, caring husband. And a strong male role model for their children.

"You're lucky," Lily murmured, her soft tone breaking into Blythe's thoughts. She was gazing out the French doors at the garden below. "My grandma Padgett always said, 'Happy is the bride the sun shines on.'"

She was smiling, but both Blythe and Cait would have had to have been deaf not to hear the sadness in her soft tone. Her words reminded everyone of how it had been raining cats and dogs the day Lily had married the scion to all those New York banking millions.

"As nice a thought as that is, Lily," Cait drawled, "I'm not sure it counts out here. Since the sun shines just about every day. And Lord knows, California's divorce rate isn't anything to brag about."

"I suppose you're right." Lily smiled and ran her palms down the front of her pleated maternity dress. "It's just a saying, after all."

"But it's still a nice thought," Blythe said, wanting to bring a smile to those pale lips.

The anniversary clock on Blythe's dresser chimed the hour, signaling it was time for the trio to go downstairs.

Blythe took a deep breath that was meant to calm, but didn't, and pressed her hands against her stomach, where giant condors had suddenly taken up residence.

"There's still time to change your mind," Cait advised, determined to give it one last shot. Having fallen head over heels in love with Sloan, she wanted both her friends to be as happy as she was.

"Don't be silly." Blythe threw back her bare shoulders, reminding Cait of a death row inmate preparing for the long walk to the electric chair. "I'm not going to disappoint all those people down there."

Cait found herself wishing for a call from the governor, offering Blythe a reprieve. When Lily gave her a puzzled, concerned look, she knew their thoughts were running along the same track.

"Better to disappoint a few friends than spend the rest of your life regretting what you should have done," Lily advised, her own expression now as grave as Cait's.

"Honestly." Blythe shook her head and managed a weak laugh. "You two are overreacting to a normal, everyday case of prewedding jitters."

She scooped up her white orchid bouquet from the bed and marched out the door. Toward her groom.

Cait took a quick glance in the mirror, assured that her makeup covered the yellowing bruises that had not yet faded. Then, exchanging another frustrated, worried look, she and Lily followed the bride downstairs.

Lily was first to walk down the white runner. Although her obviously pregnant condition drew a few murmurs— and a slight frown from the groom—most people smiled.

Cait was next. Sitting in the front row between Blythe's parents and Natalie Landis, Sloan watched the woman he loved approach on that sure, long-legged stride and decided that she'd make a stunningly beautiful bride. Which, now that they'd gotten over the hurdle of his mother, he'd already vowed would be sooner than later.

When the harpist viewed Blythe's appearance in the arbor, she broke into the wedding march. The assembled guests all turned to view the bride.

Gage, who'd been given a verbal invitation during their lunch at Le Chardonnay, was sitting on the aisle midway down the white runner. As she approached, Blythe's attention was suddenly drawn to him.

Their eyes locked. The same way they had during that brief, startling moment on his boat. But this time, instead of her mind being washed clear, as impossible as it seemed, she felt it melding with his.

You can't do this, his suddenly stormy eyes told her.

I have to, hers answered back.

You don't have to do anything, his countered on a flare of passion. *But leave with me. Now.*

I can't. Unaware that she'd stopped beside his chair,

Blythe also failed to hear the curious murmur of the assembled guests.

You can. He was holding her wary gaze to his with the sheer strength of his will. *I'll help you.*

They still hadn't said a word out loud. But it wasn't necessary. Not when their eyes and their minds were exchanging such intensely sensual messages.

Heaven help her, Blythe found herself unreasonably tempted to take Gage up on his outrageous invitation when suddenly there was a low, deepening rumble, like an approaching freight train.

Then it happened.

The massive, upward jolt beneath her feet hurled Blythe into Gage. They were both thrown violently to the ground. As if the garden were nothing more than a glass ball being shaken by the angry hand of an ancient, mythic god, the white satin-covered chairs bucked wedding guests in all directions, causing them to land on top of one another, their cries of alarm unable to be heard over the deafening roar of the trembling earth.

The water in the nearby fountain sloshed over the rim, drenching Alan who was thrown against the arbor, where he became hopelessly tangled amidst the thorny rose bush.

The violently shaking ground disoriented Lily, who felt as if she'd suddenly dived beneath the sea, in the dark. Knocked to her knees by the first jolt, she folded her arms across her distended belly in an instinctive maternal effort to protect her unborn child from nature's raging forces. Closing her eyes tightly, she began reciting prayers learned in childhood.

Time took on a strange, slow-motion feel. Sloan, who'd been hurled from his chair in the front row, attempted to make his way to Cait, whom he could see lying nearby, seemingly unconscious beneath one of a pair of white-framed French doors that had literally burst out of the house.

It was not the first earthquake Blythe had experienced. But it was the most terrifying. Because it seemed to last a lifetime. Shattered glass from the windows was raining down all around them. Unable to run, she clung to Gage, who was lying on top of her to protect her from the falling debris, and waited for the nightmare to be over.

And then, just as suddenly as it began, everything, including the ground, went deathly, silently still.

Desperate to reach Cait, Sloan pushed himself up to his feet, only to be tossed back to his knees by a second, even stronger shock.

Shouting her name, he struggled to crawl to her, feeling as if he were slogging through a mass of quivering Jell-O. Every atom of his being focused on the woman he loved, Sloan was only aware on the vaguest level of the pandemonium going on around him as he made his way, inch by painful inch, toward her.

He'd managed to reach her side just as the second tremor ceased and, pulled the door from her body, fear supplying an adrenaline rush that allowed him to toss the heavy wood frame away as if it were no heavier than a feather.

"You're going to be all right," he insisted, as if determination could make it so. He pressed a handkerchief against the gash on her forehead.

To his vast relief, her lashes fluttered. Her dazed eyes opened. "Oh, God, I thought I'd lost you." Sloan rained kisses all over her smudged face. His heart was still pounding with a rhythm that couldn't possibly be normal for anyone, but at least it no longer felt as if it were going to burst out of his chest.

"Never." She lifted a hand to his cheek, trying not to flinch when the gesture caused a shock to shoot through her wrist. Her head was throbbing painfully.

"Dammit, Cait, we belong together."

"Yes." Never in her life had she known anything to be so true.

Adrenaline was still running in his veins and Sloan was on a roll. Intent upon getting his feelings out, he didn't immediately hear her. "I understand all about your parents, but I'm not your father, or any of your stepfathers.

"I also know how you feel about people in the movie business, but I love you. And this time I'm not going to listen to any arguments. Because—"

He stopped abruptly and stared down at her. "Did you say what I think you just said?"

"Yes, Sloan, of course I'll marry you."

Relief, joy, love. They flowed through him. As Sloan touched his lips to Cait's, another aftershock hit.

"Besides," Cait managed as they were taken on yet another roller coaster ride, "I'm not about to turn down a proposal from a man who can literally make the earth move."

With a breathless laugh, Cait wrapped her arms around Sloan and clung.

COMING UP IN BACHELOR ARMS

When Blythe Fielding planned her wedding and asked her two best friends, Caitlin and Lily, to be bridesmaids, none of them had a clue a new romance was around the corner for each of them—even the bride! These entertaining, dramatic stories of friendship, mystery and love by JoAnn Ross continue the exploits of the residents of Bachelor Arms and answer one very important question: Will Blythe ever walk down the aisle? Find out in:

For Richer or Poorer (June 1995, #541)

Three Grooms and a Wedding (July 1995, #545)

Soon to move into Bachelor Arms are the heroes and heroines in books by always popular Candace Schuler and Judith Arnold. Don't miss their stories!

HARLEQUIN®

Temptation

Secret Fantasies

Do you have a secret fantasy?

Willow Evans does. But it involved independence
and solitude at the Cape Cod house she'd inherited
from her grandmother. Not being torn between two
men...who look identical...neither of whom can really
exist...who both want her. One man loves her...the
other needs her. Discover a tale of impossible love by
Lynn Michaels in #542 NIGHTWING, available in
June 1995.

Everybody has a secret fantasy. And you'll find them
all in Temptation's exciting new yearlong miniseries,
Secret Fantasies. Beginning January 1995, one book
each month focuses on the hero or heroine's innermost
romantic desires....

SF-6

HARLEQUIN®
Temptation

BACHELOR ARMS SURVEY

SET THE SCENE!

Pick your spot for the world's best marriage proposal

1. You and your love at home curled up in front of a roaring fire.
2. You and he alone on top of a mountain you've just hiked with the world spread out below you.
3. He whisks you away to a tropical island for a long weekend and proposes on the beach at sunset.
4. He pulls out a gorgeous ring at a wonderful restaurant and, after you accept, the waiters burst into song and pour champagne to the deafening applause.
5. At a surprise party for you on Valentine's Day with all your friends and family in attendance.

We want to hear from you, so please send in your response to:

In the U.S.: BACHELOR ARMS,
P.O. Box 9076, Buffalo, NY 14269-9076

In Canada: BACHELOR ARMS,
P.O. Box 637, Ft. Erie, ON L2A 5X3

Name: _____

Address:_____ City:_____

State/Prov.:_____ Zip/Postal Code:_____

Please note that all entries become the property of Harlequin and we may publish them in any publication with credit at our discretion.

HTBA2

ANNOUNCING THE

FLYAWAY VACATION SWEEPSTAKES!

This month's destination:

Beautiful SAN FRANCISCO!

This month, as a special surprise, we're offering an exciting FREE VACATION!

Think how much fun it would be to visit San Francisco "on us"! You could ride cable cars, visit Chinatown, see the Golden Gate Bridge and dine in some of the finest restaurants in America!

The facing page contains two Entry Coupons (as does every book you received this shipment). Complete and return *all* the entry coupons; **the more times you enter, the better your chances of winning!**

Then keep your fingers crossed, because you'll find out by June 15, 1995 if you're the winner! If you are, here's what you'll get:

- • Round-trip airfare for two to beautiful San Francisco!
- • 4 days/3 nights at a first-class hotel!
- • $500.00 pocket money for meals and sightseeing!

Remember: The more times you enter, the better your chances of winning!*

*NO PURCHASE OR OBLIGATION TO CONTINUE BEING A SUBSCRIBER NECESSARY TO ENTER. SEE REVERSE SIDE OR ANY ENTRY COUPON FOR ALTERNATIVE MEANS OF ENTRY.

VSF KAL

FLYAWAY VACATION
SWEEPSTAKES

OFFICIAL ENTRY COUPON

This entry must be received by: MAY 30, 1995
This month's winner will be notified by: JUNE 15, 1995
Trip must be taken between: JULY 30, 1995-JULY 30, 1996

YES, I want to win the San Francisco vacation for two. I understand the prize includes round-trip airfare, first-class hotel and $500.00 spending money. Please let me know if I'm the winner!

Name_____

Address _____ Apt. _____

City   State/Prov.   Zip/Postal Code

Account #_____

Return entry with invoice in reply envelope.

© 1995 HARLEQUIN ENTERPRISES LTD.   CSF KAL

FLYAWAY VACATION
SWEEPSTAKES

OFFICIAL ENTRY COUPON

This entry must be received by: MAY 30, 1995
This month's winner will be notified by: JUNE 15, 1995
Trip must be taken between: JULY 30, 1995-JULY 30, 1996

YES, I want to win the San Francisco vacation for two. I understand the prize includes round-trip airfare, first-class hotel and $500.00 spending money. Please let me know if I'm the winner!

Name_____

Address _____ Apt. _____

City   State/Prov.   Zip/Postal Code

Account #_____

Return entry with invoice in reply envelope.

© 1995 HARLEQUIN ENTERPRISES LTD.   CSF KAL

OFFICIAL RULES

FLYAWAY VACATION SWEEPSTAKES 3449

NO PURCHASE OR OBLIGATION NECESSARY

Three Harlequin Reader Service 1995 shipments will contain respectively, coupons for entry into three different prize drawings, one for a trip for two to San Francisco, another for a trip for two to Las Vegas and the third for a trip for two to Orlando, Florida. To enter any drawing using an Entry Coupon, simply complete and mail according to directions.

There is no obligation to continue using the Reader Service to enter and be eligible for any prize drawing. You may also enter any drawing by hand printing the words "Flyaway Vacation," your name and address on a 3"x5" card and the destination of the prize you wish that entry to be considered for (i.e., San Francisco trip, Las Vegas trip or Orlando trip). Send your 3"x5" entries via first-class mail (limit: one entry per envelope) to: Flyaway Vacation Sweepstakes 3449, c/o Prize Destination you wish that entry to be considered for, P.O. Box 1315, Buffalo, NY 14269-1315, USA or P.O. Box 610, Fort Erie, Ontario L2A 5X3, Canada.

To be eligible for the San Francisco trip, entries must be received by 5/30/95; for the Las Vegas trip, 7/30/95; and for the Orlando trip, 9/30/95.

Winners will be determined in random drawings conducted under the supervision of D.L. Blair, Inc., an independent judging organization whose decisions are final, from among all eligible entries received for that drawing. San Francisco trip prize includes round-trip airfare for two, 4-day/3-night weekend accommodations at a first-class hotel, and $500 in cash (trip must be taken between 7/30/95—7/30/96, approximate prize value—$3,500); Las Vegas trip includes round-trip airfare for two, 4-day/3-night weekend accommodations at a first-class hotel, and $500 in cash (trip must be taken between 9/30/95—9/30/96, approximate prize value—$3,500); Orlando trip includes round-trip airfare for two, 4-day/3-night weekend accommodations at a first-class hotel, and $500 in cash (trip must be taken between 11/30/95—11/30/96, approximate prize value—$3,500). All travelers must sign and return a Release of Liability prior to travel. Hotel accommodations and flights are subject to accommodation and schedule availability. Sweepstakes open to residents of the U.S. (except Puerto Rico) and Canada, 18 years of age or older. Employees and immediate family members of Harlequin Enterprises, Ltd., D.L. Blair, Inc., their affiliates, subsidiaries and all other agencies, entities and persons connected with the use, marketing or conduct of this sweepstakes are not eligible. Odds of winning a prize are dependent upon the number of eligible entries received for that drawing. Prize drawing and winner notification for each drawing will occur no later than 15 days after deadline for entry eligibility for that drawing. Limit: one prize to an individual, family or organization. All applicable laws and regulations apply. Sweepstakes offer void wherever prohibited by law. Any litigation within the province of Quebec respecting the conduct and awarding of the prizes in this sweepstakes must be submitted to the Regies des loteries et Courses du Quebec. In order to win a prize, residents of Canada will be required to correctly answer a time-limited arithmetical skill-testing question. Value of prizes are in U.S. currency.

Winners will be obligated to sign and return an Affidavit of Eligibility within 30 days of notification. In the event of noncompliance within this time period, prize may not be awarded. If any prize or prize notification is returned as undeliverable, that prize will not be awarded. By acceptance of a prize, winner consents to use of his/her name, photograph or other likeness for purposes of advertising, trade and promotion on behalf of Harlequin Enterprises, Ltd., without further compensation, unless prohibited by law.

For the names of prizewinners (available after 12/31/95), send a self-addressed, stamped envelope to: Flyaway Vacation Sweepstakes 3449 Winners, P.O. Box 4200, Blair, NE 68009.

RVC KAL